Pokémon
DETECTIVE PIKACHU ™

MOVIE NOVEL

ADAPTED BY SONIA SANDER
WRITTEN BY DAN HERNANDEZ & BENJI SAMIT

SCHOLASTIC INC.

Published by Scholastic Inc., *Publishers since 1920*. SCHOLASTIC and associated logos are trademarks and/or registered trademarks of Scholastic Inc.

ISBN 978-1-338-52942-5

10 9 8 7 6 5 4 3 2 1   19 20 21 22 23

Printed in the U.S.A.   40
First printing 2019

Designed by Carolyn Bull

CHAPTER 1

High atop a snow-covered mountain, car tires screeched out of control as a mystery driver hastily sped away from a solitary building—home to a secret science lab. Inside, dark minds were at work. The Legendary Pokémon Mewtwo, a creature of vast power and special abilities, was locked up in a containment chamber. With eyes like daggers, Mewtwo stared out of the chamber.

Mewtwo sensed the car's departure and was waiting for its chance to escape. It was fed up with being experimented on under the bright white lights of the lab. *They're outside,* thought a determined Mewtwo as it shifted in the containment chamber.

Suddenly, an automated voice from above sounded an alert. "CONDITION: RED!" The glass enclosing Mewtwo in the chamber cracked.

"We're losing power in the containment chamber!" warned the lead scientist, Dr. Laurent, as she rushed to try to manage the situation at hand.

The glass only cracked further and then exploded— sending razor-sharp shards everywhere. The lab workers ran for cover as explosions spread through the lab, one after another.

Mewtwo burst free from its chamber and shot out of the building and up into the night sky to escape. Its growl could be heard far and wide. "*OOOOAAAAHHHHHHH!*" Mewtwo hovered momentarily in the air with its arm stretched out wide, recovering from being scrunched up so long inside the containment chamber.

The driver who had raced from the lab was now recklessly racing down the mountain toward civilization— Ryme City, the bright glow in the distance. Soon, a mysterious purple orb was closely trailing the car. As the car approached a bridge, it tried to outrun the purple orb by accelerating. Without warning, the purple orb sped ahead and descended in front of the car.

BAM! The car swerved widely, out of control, trying to avoid hitting the orb. It slammed through the barrier and plummeted off the bridge.

CHAPTER 2

It was quiet as dawn awakened the rolling hills of the wilderness that was home to multitudes of Pokémon. Deep in the woods, two young adults, Tim Goodman and his childhood friend, Jack—were making their way through the overgrowth. Jack was clearly on a mission. Tim, wearing his slacks and a button-down shirt for his office job, was begrudgingly following Jack's lead. A noise from above the ravine stopped them in their tracks.

"You hear that?" whispered Jack as he peeked out of the ravine.

"Something's close," replied Tim, finally sounding intrigued by whatever adventure Jack had planned for them this morning.

"Yeah, you think?" asked Jack excitedly. "See! This is

what I'm talking about! My heart is pounding."

Tim knew exactly what Jack meant. He could feel his own heart pounding uncontrollably as a childlike excitement rushed through him.

Jack quietly pulled Tim down to peer through the tall grass. In the clearing beyond, there was a small creature wearing a mask made of bone. Tim knew exactly what it was. His face fell as he turned to Jack.

"Cubone?" Tim asked in disbelief. "We're not catching you a Pokémon, are we?"

"What?" Jack replied, pretending he didn't know what Tim was talking about.

"Tell me you didn't plan this, Jack." Tim demanded.

"Are you serious? How dare you! Of course not—come on!" Jack protested a bit too much, and then came clean. "Okay, maybe."

Annoyed with Jack for dragging him out into the wilderness at such an early hour, Tim got up and turned to walk away.

"Wait!" a guilt-ridden Jack called out. He wanted to get Tim back on board. "There was a full moon last night and my mom heard the Cubone crying its eyes out. Well, she actually thought I was having a nightmare, so she brought me a glass of warm milk."

"Dude, I thought you wanted to hang out and relive the good ol' days, like when we were kids," complained Tim.

"I do!" Jack said as he moved in front of Tim and motioned toward the Pokémon. "But just look at it." Cubone was looking up at the sky, tears streaming down its face. "That is the perfect Pokémon for you," Jack insisted.

"Jack, I'm not looking for a Pokémon. I've told you this," Tim reminded him. He wished Jack would stop harping on it—and would listen to him and let it go.

"I have thought long and hard about this," Jack continued, meaning well, but yet again ignoring Tim's wishes. "Water type is not right for you. Neither is a Fire type. But Cubone is . . ."

"Lonely," Tim finished Jack's sentence.

"Exactly! Yes," said Jack.

Lonely, Tim thought. *Just like me.* That stung a little. But he rolled his eyes, and said, "Okay. Thank you, Jack. Are there any other emotional truth-bombs you wanna drop on me?"

"Maybe later. But right now, the truth is in my hands." Jack pulled out a ball that was red on top and white on the bottom, with a black horizontal band around its center and a gray button in its middle. It was a Poké Ball. Jack and Tim both stared down at it.

Tim sighed and gave in to Jack's persistence. "Just give me the ball."

Jack handed it to him. Tim rolled his wrist around, trying to remember how it felt to catch a Pokémon. It had been a long time since he had tried—and he was no expert. Tim slowly got up and made his way into the field toward Cubone.

Jack tried to be helpful and reminded him, "Remember, catching Pokémon is not about skill. So you can do this."

Tim shot him a look. "Good pep talk!"

Jack ignored him and continued. "It has to *choose you*, too. So make it want to be your partner."

The Cubone cocked its little head to look at Tim. But it was not a welcoming look by any means. *Why am I doing this again?* Tim thought. He grudgingly—but carefully—inched his way toward the now-very-alert Cubone.

"Hey, Cubone," Tim called out gently. "What's up, buddy? You know, not everyone can pull off wearing the skull of their dead relative, but, you know, you sure can."

The Cubone made a small growl. Tim could tell that the Cubone didn't like what he had said. He hesitated, and looked back at Jack, who encouraged him to throw the Poké Ball. "Throw it like a man!"

Tim took a deep breath, reminding himself that he'd done this countless times before, and focused on the task at hand. Then, he ran and threw with an action pose reminiscent of the classic Pokémon Trainers. The Cubone saw the Poké Ball coming, and yelled, *"Cubone!"* while turning to run away . . . but the ball hit Cubone in the back of the head and bounced backward, sucking Cubone inside before landing quietly on the ground. Tim felt proud, and walked confidently over to retrieve the Poké Ball. "I did it!" he cried. "I still got it!"

But before Tim could pick up the Poké Ball, it started to rumble and shudder. "The light's not green," shouted Tim, and he slowly backed away from it. He could tell something wasn't quite right. "It still hasn't turned green yet, Jack. That's bad, right?"

"Run!" yelled Jack, who realized the Cubone hadn't accepted being captured.

Cubone burst from the broken ball and used its Bonemerang move on Tim. The bone flew through the air and blasted the dirt near Tim.

"It didn't choose me, Jack!" Tim cried as he ran across the field. "I am not its choice!"

Determined to hit Tim with its bone, Cubone chased

after him, thowing its bone at him over and over again. Finally, the bone blasted the ground under Tim's feet and sent him flying. He crashed face-first into the field. Cubone cheered as Tim slowly lifted his head and spit out a mouthful of grass.

Not long after, Jack and Tim made their way back into Leaventown, the small town where they lived. Tim wiped the dirt off of his work shirt. The morning hadn't gone quite as well as Jack had hoped. It was a complete disaster. He knew he had messed up. "That was one angry Cubone," said Jack apologetically. "It reminded me a lot of my mom."

"Apology accepted," said Tim, who knew in his heart that his friend was just trying to help him.

"So, um"—Jack hesitated nervously—"I don't know if this is going to sound corny or whatever—"

"Just say it, Jack," Tim interrupted. "I'm too tired to be angry."

"I'm worried about you," confessed Jack, hoping Tim would finally open up and talk to him.

"This again?" Tim said, rolling his eyes. He was completely over having this particular conversation with his friend.

"Okay, listen," added Jack, treading carefully. "Everyone

we know has left town, and now I'm leaving, too."

"Yeah, but that's okay," Tim reassured Jack. "You gotta do what's best for you with the time you've got. That's what I'm doing. You know, I'm crushing it at work. Gonna get a promotion real soon."

"What's the next level for an insurance appraiser?" Jack teased Tim. "Senior insurance appraiser?"

"Actually, that's two steps above where I am right now," Tim said.

"You're gonna make me throw up," Jack complained, still not understanding why Tim didn't want to get out and explore all that the world had to offer. "That's not a real thing."

Just as they reached the front door of Tim's office— Whimsmore Insurance—Tim's phone pinged. They had just regained cell service. He had five voice mails in total waiting for him. He couldn't understand why there would be so many. Who was calling him so urgently?

"Maybe it's an insurance emergency," joked Jack.

It turned out to be an emergency, but not related to his work at the insurance company. As Tim listened to his messages, his face grew more and more serious and Jack grew more and more concerned.

"Who is it?" Jack asked, regretting his joke about an emergency.

"Um, it's the Ryme City Police Department," replied Tim, still reeling from what he had just heard. "There was an accident."

CHAPTER 3

The next morning, Tim slept for most of the train ride into Ryme City. When he finally woke up, he picked up a newspaper to help him occupy the last portion of his journey. He took one look at the headline, "Detective Dies in Fiery Crash," then rolled his eyes and tossed the paper back down onto the seat.

But there was something else there to distract Tim—unfortunately. He sensed that someone else was invading his personal space, and slowly turned toward the aisle. Lickitung—a pink Pokémon—was standing so close to Tim, he could feel it breathing on him. Lickitung opened its mouth and revealed its giant tongue. Tim tensed up. He already knew what was coming next. It was inevitable with this particular Pokémon. Tim pleaded with the

Lickitung, hoping he could dissuade it from continuing. "Please don't . . ."

But the Pokémon was determined to follow through with its plan. Lickitung slowly, deliberately, and disgustingly dragged its tongue up Tim's face.

"Mm. I actually meant please *do*," Tim said sarcastically as he used his seat cover to wipe his face clean. "Thank you. Thank you. You have a very generous tongue."

Tim looked around the train car, up and down the aisle. "Does this Lickitung belong to anyone? Anybody?" But no one claimed it.

Luckily, the train ride was nearly over. As the train approached its final destination, an informational video welcoming visitors to Ryme City played on the screen in front of Tim.

The video showed a wide shot panning over the city, as a narrator talked. "*Throughout history, Pokémon have been a part of our world. Early humans used to catch them and train them to use their unique powers for the common good. This relationship evolved into what we now refer to as Pokémon battles. One man changed all of this: Howard Clifford, founder and chairman of Clifford Industries. Diagnosed with a rare degenerative disease, he resigned from running his corporation and searched the world for a cure.*"

Then an old man in a wheelchair came onto the screen

and began talking. *"And it turned out that the cure I was looking for was for me to evolve into a better version of myself. And I discovered how to do that through a partnership with Pokémon."*

The screen cut to a younger man, who said, *"And he wanted to share that discovery with the world."*

The narrator continued, *"This is what inspired Howard Clifford to build Ryme City. A place where humans and Pokémon can live side by side. Unlike other regions, where Pokémon live in the wild, here we live and work together. No battles, no Trainers, no Poké Balls. A stronger, more harmonious world."*

The man in the wheelchair smiled out from the screen. *"From all of our citizens, welcome to Ryme City."*

A few minutes later, Tim emerged from the train. Big screens around the station were playing another version of the welcome video he had just seen. He made his way through the Tahnti train station, and exited with a crowd of commuters. He felt slightly overwhelmed by the bustling scene before him, and all the sights, sounds, and smells. Ryme City was a big metropolis, and it was full of thousands of Pokémon coexisting with people in seemingly perfect harmony. Tim was used to a slow, quiet lifestyle in a small town—he was experiencing total sensory overload!

As Tim made his way through the city, still not used to the crowd, he caught himself staring at various Pokémon living their lives in the city. Machamp, a large Pokémon with four massive arms, was directing traffic at an intersection. A few streets later, he saw several little Pancham chewing on leaves in a bamboo garden as their respective human partners watched with glee.

Distracted by the sights and sounds of Ryme City, Tim shifted his attention and tried to focus back at the task at hand—getting to his destination. He checked a map on his phone, and then continued navigating his way slowly through the throngs of people and Pokémon.

Finally standing outside the Ryme City Police Department, Tim paused to catch his breath and mentally prepare himself for whatever was ahead. Inside, Tim was directed to Lieutenant Yoshida's office. A Snubbull sat on the Lieutenant's desk, staring a hole through Tim while he waited for Yoshida. It was adorable, but extremely grumpy-looking. Tim stared back, bewildered, and wondered what he'd done to make the Snubbull so unhappy. It was a welcome relief to break his stare from the Snubbull and stand up and greet Lieutenant Yoshida when he finally entered the room.

"Your dad was the best of the best. He was a legend in this precinct," Yoshida said as he greeted Tim.

"Thank you. Thank you for saying that," Tim replied, still unsure about how to feel about the whole situation.

As Yoshida took his seat, he set down a file labeled HARRY GOODMAN. Tim couldn't take his eyes off the file as he slowly sat back down in his chair.

"It was a terrible tragedy losing him and his partner," Yoshida added solemnly.

"His partner?" Tim asked. He hadn't realized his dad even had a partner.

"His Pokémon," replied Yoshida.

"Oh, I didn't know that he had one . . ." admitted Tim and then added. "I'm sorry—is yours mad at me?"

"Snubbull?" Yoshida asked, shaking his head and smiling. He stroked Snubbull's head protectively. "He may look grumpy on the outside, but I assure you he is adorable on the inside."

Tim wasn't entirely sure he believed Yoshida as he took in Snubbull's grumpy face again.

Yoshida leaned back, shifting gears, hoping to engage Tim. "If you don't mind me asking, how come you don't have a Pokémon? I thought I remember Harry saying you wanted to be a Pokémon Trainer when you were young."

"Yeah, that didn't really work out," Tim said. "I work in insurance now, so . . ."

"I see," said Yoshida, clearly disappointed. "But, Tim . . . please don't put this all on yourself. No one should go through this type of thing alone. If you're anything like your dad—"

"I'm not. I was really raised by my grandmother," Tim interrupted. He had even surprised himself with how abruptly he responded. Clearly, Yoshida had hit a nerve. The two men sat in silence for a moment. "Do you have the spare keys for his apartment?" Tim asked. "I should go wrap things up there."

Seeing that Tim was all business, Yoshida quickly handed him the keys and gave him his dad's address.

"I can take you over if you want," offered Yoshida.

"No—nope. I'm good," said Tim, itching to leave and get it all over with. "Thank you so much."

"Tim," Yoshida added as Tim stood to leave. "This job—being a police detective—it demands a lot. But you were on his mind every day. He loved you more than anything in the world."

Tim was caught a little off guard by what Yoshida had shared about his dad—but only for a moment. He quickly regained his composure and didn't waste any time making his exit.

"It was nice to meet you, Lieutenant," he said as he walked out.

CHAPTER 4

Tim walked over to his dad's apartment, making his way from busy streets crowded with high-rises to a quieter neighborhood of industrial warehouses and dingy side streets. On one of these side streets was his dad's place, a low-rent apartment building. It was starting to get dark.

He hustled up to the entrance, and then paused. He was sure he could feel someone watching him. Tim turned around, but saw only a confused-looking Psyduck holding a newspaper and staring directly at him from across the street. That was a little odd. But Tim quickly turned back and opened the door to the apartment building.

Inside the rundown lobby, a porter and his Treecko Pokémon partner were fast asleep behind the reception desk. "Excuse me," called out Tim. But the porter continued to sleep. Only the Treecko woke up, and it wasn't happy about it. So Tim took it upon himself to find his way around.

He located the mailbox labeled H. GOODMAN and opened it with his key. It was stuffed with mail. Sensing someone behind him, Tim whirled around and was startled to find the same Psyduck from outside standing uncomfortably close to him. Tim wondered why it was here, and who it belonged to. He took a good look around the lobby but didn't see anything out of the ordinary—except the Psyduck.

"*Psyduck, psyduck, psyduck, psyduck, psyduck. Psyduck,*" the Psyduck babbled.

"Are you trying to rob me or just annoy me?" demanded Tim.

A mysterious-looking young woman wearing sunglasses suddenly stepped out of the shadows and answered Tim's question. "He's with me. We need to talk. We've been waiting to see who would open up that mailbox." She and Tim stared at each other for a moment, then she took another step closer, and continued, "You just walked into quite a story. A story like this spreads fear, and they're afraid of fear. But I don't fear fear. I walk the walk and I talk the talk, and I'm willing to do whatever it takes to get the honest scoop, and that's the hard truth."

Tim was stunned. "I'm sorry, who are you?" he asked.

"Lucy Stevens, reporter for CNM," she said.

"Oh!" Tim said, surprised. "You seem kind of young for that."

Lucy grimaced, then admitted, "I work for the CNM blog making Pokémon listicles all day, okay? Like 'Top 10 Cutest Pokémon.'"

"Yeah, my grandma loves those!" Tim responded.

"Well, news flash—all Pokémon are cute!" Lucy said, then rolled her eyes. "Such a waste of time for someone with my nose for a story."

Psyduck interjected, agitated. *"Psyduck, psyduck, psy-duuuck!"*

Lucy crouched down by it and said sweetly, "Not now, Psyduck—I'm working on a source."

Tim tried to sneak past Lucy toward the stairs while she was calming down Psyduck, but she was too quick. She stood up, blocking his path, and whipped out her cell phone. Shoving it in Tim's face, she clicked on the recorder. "I'm gonna need you to go on the record and tell me every-thing you know about Harry Goodman," she said. "Harry was on to something big, real big . . . and then all of a sud-den his car crashed over a bridge? I think not. Something's rotten and I'm gonna get to the bottom of it."

"Hey, look, I barely knew the guy. I haven't seen him in years," confessed Tim.

Lucy looked suspicious, and asked forcefully, "Where's your Pokémon partner?"

"I don't have one. Why does everyone keep asking me that?" demanded Tim.

Lucy brought the phone recorder toward her face and said into it, "Loner. Probably hiding something."

Tim turned and started to head up the stairs. Lucy called after him, "Listen to me—I may only be an unpaid intern, but I can smell a story, and I'm going to find it."

"Okay, you do that," suggested Tim.

Lucy clicked her recorder off and made her way out. "Come on, Psyduck. Let's go."

Tim glanced over his shoulder at her as he continued up the stairs. Lucy was persistent, but also cute—she had definitely caught his attention in more ways than one.

Once inside his dad's apartment, Tim took a moment to take in his surroundings. It was a dark, rundown two-bedroom that was more office than home. Tim heard a voice speaking, and wondered who was inside his dad's apartment, but on closer investigation, it turned out someone had just left on the television. An old black-and-white detective movie was playing. He remembered how much his dad had liked those.

Tim turned off the television. The silence was deafening, so he began to look around the place. One wall was covered in awards from the city for Harry's police work. A pile of tattered gumshoe fiction sat on the coffee table. Tim absentmindedly ran his finger across the spines and then crossed the room to his dad's desk. He leafed through all the notes and paperwork sitting on top. He noticed a newspaper clipping about the "Ancient Mew," and when he picked it up to look, he saw that underneath it was a glass vial filled with a purple liquid.

Tim carefully lifted the vial to examine it, and saw it was fitted with a high-tech black cap. Suddenly, he accidentally triggered a button on the cap, and a cloud of purple gas was released into the air. Tim inhaled it, which made him cough and cough. He ran over to the window and threw it open to get some fresh air.

The purple gas floated out of the window toward some Aipom that were hanging off a neon sign outside the apartment building by the hands at the end of their tails. As soon as the breeze wafted the purple gas over to them, the Aipom were immediately affected. Their eyes dilated, and they became wild and crazed.

Tim couldn't see the Aipom. He dropped the glass vial back on the desk and stepped away from the window as his lungs cleared. "What is this stuff?!" he wondered.

Turning his attention back to the rest of the apartment, Tim checked out one of the two bedrooms. Inside, a card on the bureau caught his eye. It was a "Happy 21st Birthday" card. Tim realized his dad was planning on showing up for his birthday after all. Inside the card, there was a train ticket and a message from his dad.

Dear Tim, I can do better if you give me a chance. I will always have a place for you to stay.

The ticket brought back a flood of memories from when Tim was ten. He was standing at the train station in his small hometown with his grandma and refusing to get on the train to visit his dad in the big city.

". . . and your father will pick you up from the train station," Tim recalled his grandma telling him.

"I'm not going!" Tim had insisted. "I don't want to go. This is home. I want to stay here with you, Grandma."

In the present, the second bedroom of his dad's apartment brought back even more memories for Tim. It was decorated for a teenager who loved Pokémon. The walls were covered with photos of Tim over the years and the headboard on the bed matched the one he'd had when he'd been little: it had yellow Pikachu ears. Tim sat on the edge of the bed as his emotions started to overwhelm him. "Oh, man," he sighed, realizing how much work his dad must have put into the room.

Tim flashed back to a memory in his childhood bedroom. It was raining outside and his grandma was standing in the doorway to Tim's room, talking to him. "This is the most important day of my life," Tim exclaimed, feeling equally sad and frustrated.

"I know, Tim," his grandma said, trying to comfort him. "But your mother had to see the doctor. It couldn't wait."

Tim remembered sitting in his bedroom again, looking out his window into the rain and watching his father get out of a car. As his father came into the house, Tim crouched down at the top of the stairs. His grandma cried and hugged his dad, and Tim looked down at them in shock. That was just before he learned that his mother had died.

A noise in the living room drew Tim's attention away from the past and back to the present and the apartment. He wiped the tears from his eyes and walked out to the living room. "Is someone there?" Tim called out a bit nervously. "Hello?"

There was no response. Tim looked all around the

room, but there was no one there—or so he thought. Suddenly, a yellow blur darted across the floor, knocking over a lamp. "Ow, lamp! Oh, ah!" a voice cried out. A large shadow of the intruder covered most of the wall.

Panicked and scared, Tim looked for a weapon. The best he could find was a stapler, which he held up like a gun. "Okay, okay, okay . . . Whoever you are . . . I know how to use this!"

Out of the shadows stepped . . . a little Pikachu, wearing a detective hat.

"Oh, it's a Pikachu?" Tim sighed with relief. "Hey, little guy, how did you . . . get in here?"

"I know you can't understand me," the Pikachu said slowly in a surprisingly deep voice, kind of like the detective from the movie that had been playing. "But put down the stapler, or I will electrocute you."

"Did you just talk?!" Tim exclaimed. He was so shocked, he dropped the stapler.

Detective Pikachu couldn't believe it, either. "Whoa! Did you just understand me? Wait—wait, wait, wait, wait. That is heavy eye contact right there. You heard me."

"No, no, no. No, no, no. Stop, stop, stop, stop!" Tim shook his head, refusing to believe the impossible— that he could actually understand a Pokémon.

"Yes, you did! This is amazing," yelled Pikachu, excitedly. "You can understand me? I've been so lonely!"

The two stood there for a moment staring at each other—taking it all in. Tim's stomach turned over.

"I'm going to throw up. I'm going to throw up," Tim repeated to himself.

"No!" Pikachu cried. "Kid, I need your help. I'm in serious trouble—I need you to listen."

Tim turned to the open window for some fresh air . . . and came face-to-face with an Aipom. One of the Aipom who had been hit with the purple gas just a short time ago. It came through the window, jumping onto the desk.

Pikachu addressed the Aipom. "Excuse me, Aipom— we're having a private conversation here!"

Tim yelled at Pikachu, "Stop talking! You are a hallucination!"

"*You're* a hallucination," Detective Pikachu replied.

Tim was overwhelmed. "You! Out! Shoo! Go!" he shouted at the Aipom.

Detective Pikachu was sure that something was off about the Aipom. Pikachu warned Tim, "I'd tread lightly there, chief. That Aipom don't look right."

Pikachu was right: the Aipom started to attack Tim.

"Hey! Hey, you! Get off him, whack job!" Detective

Pikachu cried. "Get up, kid. He's coming back around!" Pikachu bounded over the kitchen counter and tried to coach Tim through his tussle with the Aipom. "Okay, here's what you wanna do. Okay. You wanna bite him. You wanna scream. Okay, I'm gonna get a knife."

Pikachu grabbed a large kitchen knife but Tim begged him not to use it as he struggled, muffled under the Aipom, "Nah-tha-knife!"

Then, the Aipom swung Tim around the room like a rag doll. Tim crashed into every piece of furniture in the place.

"Okay, bad idea with the knife. I'll find something else," Pikachu said. He tried to think of the best way to save Tim. Finally, Pikachu found a melon and tossed it at the Aipom. It dropped Tim to grab the melon and gobble it up.

"He was just a hungry little guy," Detective Pikachu said—but then more crazed Aipom appeared on the windowsill of the apartment. "C'mon, kid, let's move!" Pikachu cried.

Tim and Pikachu ran out of the apartment into the hallway—but there were crazed Aipom there, too, coming up the stairs.

Pikachu ran through Tim's legs. "To the roof!" he cried.

As Tim tried to follow Pikachu, the Aipom grabbed at his feet. By the time he got to the roof, he had already lost one shoe. Tim and Pikachu burst out of the roof door, then slammed it shut behind them. The pack of Aipom pounded on the door.

"That's a brilliant idea!" cried Pikachu. "Hold the door! I'll find us a way down!"

"What?!" exclaimed Tim. How was he supposed to manage holding back the pack of Aipom by himself?

Pikachu took off—leaving Tim straining to keep the door closed. But he could only hold it for so long. Two seconds later, the pack of Aipom burst through the door, sending Tim flying. Pikachu escaped through a small hole that only he could fit through, leaving the pack of Aipom to turn on Tim.

"Okay, kid," began Pikachu, thinking that Tim was right behind him. "This wa—Kid? Where'd he go? Ohh . . ."

As soon as Detective Pikachu realized that Tim was still out fighting off the Aipom, he turned back to help Tim out. "Run like the wind! Blazing speed! Hmm . . . I feel like you don't understand the fundamental concept of running away," commented Pikachu as he watched Tim struggle to lose the pack of Aipom.

Tim darted in the opposite direction as the Aipom

chased him and grabbed his jacket and remaining shoe.

"That's right, lose the jacket if it's holding you back!" Detective Pikachu called out.

Now dressed in just a T-shirt, pants, and socks, Tim spotted Pikachu on the far side of the building waiting impatiently for him to catch up. Next to Pikachu was a long cylindrical vinyl debris chute hanging off the side of the building. "All right, we're jumping down here," Pikachu told Tim.

"I'm not going in the trash chute!" Tim said.

"Let me know how it goes with the crazy Pokémon!" Pikachu replied.

Tim was absolutely, one hundred percent against jumping into the trash chute—until the Aipom closed in on him again. Tim quickly realized there was nowhere to go but down. So he reluctantly hopped down the chute after Pikachu, right as the Aipom grabbed his pants.

"Wheeeee!" Pikachu enjoyed the wild ride down.

"Whoooaaa!" Tim absolutely did not. He landed in a dumpster below with a bone-crushing *whomp!* To make matters worse, he was lying in the dumpster in only a T-shirt and boxers. Tim opened his eyes to find a tiny yellow face staring down at him. "Way to stick the landing, kid," Pikachu said.

Unbeknownst to Tim, the Aipom that had been

chasing him had turned back to normal. But Tim was too busy racing through the street in his boxer shorts, waving his arms frantically, trying to warn all the pedestrians and their Pokémon partners about the rabid Aipom. "Look out! Run! Go! Go! Go!" Tim cried, pointing at the Aipom making their way out of the alley. But Tim looked so crazy, everyone turned their heads away and avoided eye contact. Finally, realizing the mysterious gas had worn off and the Aipom had calmed down and returned to normal, Tim calmed down and managed to retrieve his pants.

But he was still reeling from the fact that he could hear and understand Pikachu. How was that possible? Could anyone else understand him?

Tim asked a couple walking by if they could hear Pikachu, too. The girl said, "Yeah we can! '*Pika, pika, pika.*' He's adorable!"

"They can't understand me, kid," Detective Pikachu insisted, trying to be patient. Tim was still wrapping his head around the idea that only he could understand Pikachu.

"It's me . . . It's that stuff that I put up my nose . . ." Tim rattled on in a wild and crazy manner, trying to make sense of what was happening to him. "No, it's not like that, It was a gas; I was huffing a gas . . ." Tim explained to the same couple, who might have been a bit concerned by Tim

29

before, but now were outright afraid. The guy put a protective arm around his girlfriend, and the two got away from Tim as fast as they possibly could. "Accidentally! I was accidentally huffing gas!" Tim shouted at them.

Detective Pikachu noticed that Tim's antics were beginning to draw attention from a nearby police officer. He quickly sidled up to Tim and led him in the opposite direction. "Ix-nay on the gas-nay," Pikachu warned Tim. "Unless you want Johnny Law to give you a one–way ticket to jail. Let's move."

They continued walking down the street. Pikachu had to hustle to keep up with Tim. "This is a first for me, too, kid," said Pikachu. "I try to talk to people all the time, but all they hear is '*Pika, pika.*' They pat me, or they kiss me, or they stick a finger in me. It's really gross."

"Anyone? Can no one hear him?!" Tim continued to call out and challenge people on the street. "Can you hear him talking? Can you hear him saying words?"

"What are you not getting here, kid?" asked Pikachu, starting to get frustrated. "You're the only one who can hear me. It's like destiny."

"It's not destiny!" Tim insisted.

Detective Pikachu was done trying to figure out why Tim could understand him. Instead, he asked why Tim was in Harry's apartment. When he heard that Tim was Harry's son, he took off his hat and revealed the tag on the inside. It read, "If lost, return to Harry Goodman."

Tim couldn't believe it. He was in total shock. "*You're* Harry's Pokémon partner?!"

"You want a coffee?" Pikachu suggested to Tim. 'Cause I could use a coffee. I mean, that's—yeah, let's get a coffee. Come on."

CHAPTER 5

Detective Pikachu took Tim to the Hi-Hat Cafe, and convinced Tim to sit down with him and compare notes. Tim had calmed down enough to clean himself up a bit from his fall into the dumpster. Pikachu guzzled coffee greedily as they sat at the counter.

Pikachu confessed that he'd woken up in the middle of nowhere with a heavy case of amnesia. "The only clue to my past is Harry's name and address in this hat. So I made my way to the apartment, and that's when I found you! And your stapler gun. I don't know. Maybe Harry got in too deep."

"Deep in what?" Tim wanted to know.

"You know, mixed up with the wrong crowd, that kind of thing. Happens to the best of us. The debts pile up, the walls close in. Right becomes wrong, wrong becomes wrong," Pikachu elaborated.

Tim noticed that people were starting to stare at him because he was actually carrying on a conversation with a Pokémon. Tim pulled out his phone and started to pretend he was on a call.

"Wait—what're you—who are you calling?" asked Pikachu, a little offended that Tim had pulled out his phone mid-conversation.

"No one. Yeah, yeah, no that sounds great. That sounds great," Tim said into his phone, continuing his charade until people stopped staring.

"Wait, I'm confused," admitted Pikachu, not understanding what Tim was doing by pretending to be on the phone. "Are you hearing other voices besides mine?"

Tim shook his head no. "All I want to know is why I can understand you," Tim answered.

"Can't help you there, kid," Pikachu admitted.

Tim took a deep breath. "Okay, so you're a talking Pikachu, with no memories, who's addicted to caffeine."

"I can stop whenever I want," insisted Pikachu, ordering another round of coffee from the Ludicolo barista. "These are just choices. Look, I'm a great detective, but I can't solve my own mystery. I have no memory!"

"Then how do you even know that you're a detective?" Tim asked skeptically.

"Well, that," Pikachu explained, "I can feel that in my jellies."

"What is that?" asked Tim.

"It's that—jellies," repeated Pikachu. "You know— you feel it when you really believe in something despite everyone telling you you're wrong. Which is why I need to find Harry. He's the key to my past."

That was when Tim filled in Pikachu. "Well, I've got some bad news for you, 'cause Harry's dead."

Detective Pikachu spit out his coffee in disbelief, then climbed up on the counter and stood face-to-face with Tim. "No. No. No. Harry ain't dead. Just 'cause the cops say he's dead, doesn't mean he's dead. Did they find a body? Did the report also say that I was dead? 'Cause if I'm still alive and kicking, that means that Harry's out there, too. Case closed. But still open until I solve it."

Tim realized that Pikachu had a good point. He slowly put away his phone. "Okay, I'll bite. Solve what?" Tim asked Pikachu, who was pacing back and forth on the counter.

"Oh, I'm glad you're gonna bite. All right, here it is . . . Harry faked his own death. OR somebody else faked

Harry's death. OR Harry faked somebody else's death. That last one doesn't work at all, but the first two, those are real contenders," Pikachu rambled on.

But Tim wasn't impressed. And he was ready to go home. He said goodbye and headed out the door. Detective Pikachu scurried after Tim and tried to convince him to stay. "Hold up a sec—we're gonna need each other!" he said.

Tim spun around, tired of having Pokémon forced upon him over and over again. "No! We don't," Tim said, sharply. "I don't need a Pokémon. Period. Got it?"

"Then what about a world-class detective? Because if you wanna find your pops, I'm your best bet," persisted Pikachu.

Tim finally snapped. He'd had enough. "I think a world-class detective oughta have figured out by now that I'm not here to find my father. I'm here to say goodbye!"

Tim stiffened, uncomfortably. He was surprised at how much he had just revealed about himself to Pikachu. But he still wasn't interested in sticking around. Tim took a big step over Pikachu and kept walking.

Detective Pikachu wasn't willing to give up so easily. He continued to pursue Tim. "Look, you can talk to humans. I can talk to Pokémon. We can talk to each other. This doesn't usually happen, kid! It has to mean something!

There's magic that brought us together, and that magic is called hope. Hope that Harry is still alive."

Something in Tim shifted. Pikachu picked up on it. "Ohh, you feel it in your jellies, don't 'cha?"

"There's nothing in my jellies," insisted Tim.

Pikachu couldn't help smiling. "We're going to do this—you and me."

"I can't bel—ugh." Tim sighed, finally giving up. "I will meet you here tomorrow morning."

Tim figured he was rid of Pikachu at least for the night, but as he headed in the direction of the apartment, Pikachu was still following him. The curiosity got the better of him and Tim finally asked, "Where are you going?"

"To my apartment," Pikachu stated, as if it were totally obvious.

"What do you mean, *your* apartment?" Tim wanted to know. After a bit of back and forth, they finally came to an agreement to share the apartment for the night. "What am I doing? What am I doing?" Tim muttered to himself, having a hard time believing he had actually agreed to work with a Pokémon.

CHAPTER
6

Back upstairs in the apartment, Pikachu was in Tim's bedroom rummaging through items on the desk and making a lot of noise. "Dust everywhere. No fingerprints. Doesn't add up . . . Clues, clues, where are the clues . . ."

Tim walked in wearing a pair of his father's pajamas. "What is going on in here?"

"I'm searching the joint. Looking for clues to my pa— is this your room?" Pikachu asked, getting sidetracked.

Tim said, "No." He knew what Detective Pikachu was angling at, but he didn't say anything more.

"Does Harry have other children?" Pikachu asked, pressing the matter.

"No . . ." Tim said before relenting and telling Pikachu what he wanted to know: "He wanted me to live here when

I was a kid. So he made it look like my childhood room."

Pikachu hopped up on the bed and studied the headboard shaped like his ears. "Should we talk about the fact that your childhood bed is a Pikachu bed?"

"It's just a coincidence," Tim said, not wanting Pikachu to make a big deal about it.

"I'm sorry, can you speak up? I can't hear you. I've never been so flattered and creeped out at the same time. Are you going to make me into a lampshade?" Pikachu teased, not being able to resist letting it go quite yet. Pikachu hopped back onto the desk. "All these Pokémon cards and the battle posters . . . there's a connection, isn't there? You love Pokémon!"

"No!" Tim insisted.

But Pikachu didn't believe him one bit. "Yeah, yeah, you do."

"That was a long time ago. Before my father moved to the city and spent more time with Pokémon than his own son," Tim admitted, revealing more than he'd intended about why he gave up Pokémon for good.

"Mm, yeah, yeah, blame it on your dad," Pikachu said as he picked up a framed picture of a beautiful woman. "Look, what about this? There are pictures of her all over the apartment. She's obviously connected to Harry. She might know me. She could be a lead."

"No. She's not," Tim shook his head, sadly, and took the photo away from Pikachu. "That's my mom. She passed away when I was eleven."

"Oh . . . I'm sorry," said Pikachu. "I didn't realize."

"Thanks. Now I've gotta get some sleep. I am exhausted," Tim admitted. "Tomorrow morning, I'm gonna take you to Yoshida so we can get some answers."

CHAPTER
7

Thanks to the antics of the crazed Aipom the night before, Tim had nothing to wear the next morning. He dug through his father's closet and found a white T-shirt, jeans, boots, and a bomber jacket. He looked at himself in the mirror. Wearing his dad's clothes, he felt like he was one step closer to finding out about the father he barely knew.

Out in the living room, Tim tripped over a box and fell into Pikachu's clues—piles of Post-its, newspaper clippings, and a map of Ryme City with various pins in it. The place was an absolute mess! Tim stood up and looked around the room in horror. "What is all this?" he asked.

"Ah! My clues!" cried Pikachu as he rushed forward to reorganize his disturbed piles. "Hard work—that's what this is. And by the way, we can't go to Yoshida. Not until we know who we can trust. So put my clues back in order, would ya?"

"Those aren't clues. This is the work of a serial killer," Tim said, shaking his head.

Pikachu hopped onto a tabletop and paced across the clues covering it. "They're almost clues. I'm trying to jog my memory, retrace my steps. It helps me to see it all laid out. That's how I found this . . ."

Pikachu held up the glass vial that had held the purple gas, which Tim had discovered on Harry's desk the day before.

"Smell my finger," Detective Pikachu insisted.

"I would never smell your finger," Tim replied, revolted.

"Coward," Pikachu retorted, then turned back to the vial. "I smelled this 'R' stuff on those Aipom when they attacked us yesterday."

Pikachu handed Tim the vial. Tim could just make out the barely detectable "R" engraved on the side of it.

Pikachu continued, "See I'm thinking, Harry caught a break in the case, forcing our shadowy kingpin to send out hired goons to deliver the big hush-hush. We need to retrace Harry's steps, either solve the case ourselves or get far enough along that this A-number-one bad guy has to reveal himself or herself. So what is the way in, huh? The answer is in this room."

Tim began to protest that the room was not the answer: It was just a fire hazard full of junk and papers and newspapers! But then a newspaper article about the upcoming CNM Pokémon Parade caught his eye. "Wait a minute. I literally just met someone. She was a junior reporter at CNM. She was doing a story on Harry. I think she knows more than she let on."

"A-haha! The smart ones always do. We gotta go down to her work and press her," Pikachu announced.

It was a lead! That was just what they needed. Pikachu hopped off the desk and climbed onto Tim's shoulder as he headed for the door. But very quickly, Tim set Pikachu right back down on the ground again. "Nope. No, we're not doing that."

"Fine, I'll walk," complained Pikachu. "I'm trying to get in a hundred thousand steps this hour."

CHAPTER
8

Pikachu and Tim found Lucy at the CNM building waiting to interview Howard Clifford, the visionary icon behind Ryme City, and his son, Roger, president of CNM and chairman of Clifford Industries. The father and son were in the middle of shooting a commercial for the CNM Pokémon Parade, and Tim and Detective Pikachu stood in the back and watched.

While the camera was rolling, Howard and Roger were all smiles as they finished each other's sentences. Roger was seated next to Howard's high-tech wheelchair, and their message was delivered perfectly.

"Together, in the spirit of harmony, we're throwing the largest parade that Ryme City has ever seen. You won't want to miss it! So this weekend, we invite the people and the Pokémon to be there: a celebration of the harmony between humans and Pokémon."

But the instant the camera's stopped rolling, the niceties were forgotten, and their true feelings were revealed. Roger was fuming.

"'Visionary Icon'?" he said sarcastically. "Really, Dad? Is there an unabridged version where you cure cancer?"

Howard didn't answer his son. Instead, he drove away his wheelchair. A Ditto transformed into a stagehand and assisted Howard off the stage.

"Oh, that's right. Yep. Turn your back on me like you always did," Roger mumbled after him.

As Howard wheeled away, Lucy rushed over to Roger and brought him coffee. "Mr. Clifford! Mr. Clifford, I may have a story for you. I've heard rumors of Pokémon attacking people, but there's been no mainstream coverage. I think that—"

While Lucy was talking, Roger Clifford pulled out his designer sunglass case and obsessively wiped down his giant, ugly sunglasses. Then he rudely cut off Lucy before she could finish. "I'm sorry, we're not a tabloid, which means we don't report on rumors, gossip, or hearsay. It's not news if it can't be verified. You want a story? Find a source!"

Deflated, Lucy turned to leave. Then she spotted Tim and her eyes narrowed. A source! She marched toward Tim. "What are you doing here, Tim Goodman?"

"Here she comes. Try to look deep," Pikachu whispered to Tim as Lucy approached.

Tim turned to Lucy. "Yeah, I know this seems weird that I'm here, but I actually needed to ask you something."

Lucy told him it wasn't a good time to talk. She was about to turn and leave when Pikachu slurped his coffee very loudly, catching Lucy's attention. She looked down at Pikachu, but heard only *"Pika, pika!"* when he talked. Lucy scratched behind Pikachu's ears.

"You found yourself a Pokémon partner!" she said to Tim.

"Mmm . . . not exactly—no," Tim replied. He was eager to get back to the question he'd wanted to ask Lucy. He didn't want her to get away before he had a chance to find out what she knew. "I found something in my father's desk," Tim explained, holding up the vial. "Nearly choked me to death. I was wondering if you—"

Lucy's eyes widened as she hastily shoved the vial away from anyone else's sight. "No, not here. In my office."

Tim followed her, and Pikachu jumped on Tim's leg to

catch a ride. But, once again, Tim wasn't having it. He shook Pikachu off as he walked.

Lucy's office was not so much of an office as it was a tiny office-supply room. Her "desk" was an open filing cabinet drawer with a laptop propped on it. They all squeezed inside, and Tim and Pikachu stood pressed up against the wall. "This is great," Pikachu said sarcastically. "This isn't an office—it's a coffin with pencils."

Psyduck stood in the corner. "*Psyduck?*" it said to Pikachu.

"Yeah, that's right," answered Pikachu proudly. "I can talk to the kid; the kid can talk to me. We're gifted." Psyduck looked confused, and Pikachu turned to Tim. "You didn't tell me she has a Psyduck," he said. "Just letting you know, these things explode when they're stressed!"

"*Psyduck, psyduck, psyduck . . .*" Psyduck started to wind itself up, and Pikachu tried to get it to relax.

Lucy dug around behind her filing cabinet desk, and finally found what she was looking for in a drawer. She pulled out empty glass vials identical to the one Tim and Pikachu brought from Harry's apartment.

"Where did you find these?" asked Tim.

"Word on the street was your father had an informant near the docks. I went there to snoop around, and that's where I found the vials," Lucy explained, pointing to an area on a city map pinned to the wall. "But the docks can be dangerous. They're not the sort of place you want to visit alone at night."

Tim didn't have time for Lucy's advice. He thanked her for the intel, then headed out, confident he could handle the docks on his own.

CHAPTER 9

Fog rolled into the deserted, eerie streets surrounding the docks. But Tim was distracted by Detective Pikachu, who was riding on his shoulders. Tim wasn't happy about it.

"There are other ways for you to get around," he complained. "This is humiliating!"

"Every step for you is a thousand for me, and my lungs are the size of grapes," explained Pikachu. "We need to get some ground rules if this partnership is going to work."

But Tim still wasn't sold on the partnership idea. "You're not my partner," he said.

"Mentor, sensei, master—whatever you wanna call it. I'm fine with all of those," added Pikachu. Tim, however, was still not okay with any of those options.

"What if it wasn't the gas? What if it's hereditary, huh?"

asked Tim. "What if Harry could understand your annoying voice, too?"

"You don't need to be able to talk to us for us to understand. We can feel what you're saying," explained Pikachu. "You have to be open to the experience. Try it sometime."

"Yeah, I'd rather not," admitted Tim. "I've got my plate full talking to you."

Just then, a shadow moving on the side of a building caught Tim's attention. It looked like a small, oddly shaped person. "What is that?" he asked.

"Silent but deadly," confessed Pikachu. "Apologies. My tummy's bad from all the coffee."

"No! Get off!" cried Tim as a rotten odor hit him. Then he pointed toward the building. "I meant *that*."

Now they could see it was a Mr. Mime—"Silent but annoying," according to Pikachu. The Mr. Mime became alarmed at the sight of them.

"Does he recognize you?" Tim asked Detective Pikachu. "I think he recognizes you!"

"Well, I was Harry's partner so I would have been with him . . ." began Pikachu, and then he and Tim looked at each other slowly as they both put two and two together at the same time. "Harry's informant is a Pokémon! Get him!"

Mr. Mime took off running. But since the Mr. Mime

was only *miming* running at high speed, Tim and Pikachu easily caught up to it. Then Mr. Mime reacted by jumping onto a motorcycle and zooming off . . . but again, it was just miming. There was no actual motorcycle, and Mr. Mime was staying in one place.

"Oh, he's on a bike. Come on! He thinks he's getting away. Quick! Get in front of him. Cut him off!" Pikachu encouraged Tim.

Tim reluctantly stepped directly in front of the Mr. Mime, which then mimed crashing its bike in slow motion. "Oh no! He's going down hard, Tim. Should've worn a helmet. I hope he makes it," Pikachu said.

"Come on, this is ridiculous!" cried Tim, keen to uncover some real answers.

Pikachu and Tim took Mr. Mime into an empty warehouse to question him. They found a lamp to shine on the Pokémon, which sat on an invisible chair with one leg crossed over the other.

Before they started talking to the Mr. Mime, Pikachu whispered to Tim, "I'm good cop. You're bad cop."

Tim rolled his eyes. "We're not cops."

"Well, you're bigger and tougher-looking than I am. Stand up straight!" Pikachu said. Tim reluctantly did so, and they faced Mr. Mime.

"Listen up. We got ways to make you talk . . . or mime," Pikachu growled. "So tell us what we wanna know. Why was Harry Goodman here and what did it have to do with the vial of 'R'?"

Tim flashed Mr. Mime a glimpse of the glass vial.

Mr. Mime mimed opening a can, followed by pushing outward in front of itself. Then it pointed at Pikachu. Pikachu was furiously trying to decode the meaning of the miming, but Tim understood right away.

"It's saying you can shove it," Tim said. That made Pikachu lose it and charge at Mr. Mime—but Mr. Mime brought its hands up to mime an invisible wall, and Pikachu slammed into the wall as if it were solid. Tim cracked a smile. His childhood knowledge of Pokémon was coming back to him. "Oh yeah, Mr. Mime has the power to make invisible walls."

"Yes, I know," said a disgruntled Pikachu with a sigh. "I happen to be a Pokémon, too, remember?"

"Look, Harry figured this guy out somehow," Tim said. "I think the trick is getting inside his head."

Mr. Mime happily mimed pouring itself a glass of water and drinking it with satisfaction as it watched Tim and Pikachu from behind its invisible wall.

"I have an idea," said Tim. He stepped up to the

invisible wall and mimed opening an invisible door. To Pikachu's surprise, Tim gained access to Mr. Mime's space.

"Yeah," Tim said confronting a suddenly not-so-confident Mr. Mime. "I'm in your space now. You don't like this so much, do you?"

Tim mimed twisting open a bottle and then mimed dousing a cringing Mr. Mime with the liquid inside the bottle. Pikachu had a hard time following what was going on behind the invisible wall. At first, he thought Tim poured salt all over Mr. Mime in order to cook it. But Tim shook his head, and Pikachu kept guessing. His guesses were so wild and crazy and far from reality that Tim started getting frustrated. Even Mr. Mime couldn't take it any longer and started to also mime what was happening. Finally, the mimes started to make sense to Pikachu.

"You're pouring gasoline on Mr. Mime?" asked Pikachu. Mr. Mime gave Pikachu a thumbs-up. "Oh, I like this. I like it very much." Pikachu took large, exaggerated steps backward, as if getting clear of the spilled gasoline. Tim flicked his hand, indicating he was lighting a match. Mr. Mime frantically blew out the invisible match.

"All right," Tim said impatiently. "You want to play that game? I can play that game."

Tim mimed pouring the gasoline on the floor around

Mr. Mime, and then creating a trail of it leading back out the door Tim had opened in Mr. Mime's invisible wall. He remained outside the wall, while Mr. Mime remained inside.

Mr. Mime suddenly looked spooked—Tim had lit an invisible match. "Oh. Oh, I smell what you're stepping in," said Pikachu, referring to the invisible gasoline. "That's right, Mr. Mime. You're about to be Mr. Melt, unless you start talking."

Not wanting to be burned, Mr. Mime panicked. It made motions as if it were dealing cards.

"Cards. Playing cards. Poker," guessed Pikachu.

"No." said Tim. "I think Mr. Mime is talking about the 'R.'"

Mr. Mime pointed at Tim: YES! Then he dealt cards again.

"Someone was handing out 'R'? Use your body words. Where?" demanded Pikachu.

Mr. Mime mimed "house" in a few different ways.

Pikachu tried to make sense of the mimes again, but grew increasingly frustrated. "Circle house? Moon house. Moon. House. Enough with the games! Say it! Just say it!"

Tim realized that Pikachu was about to lose it and stepped in to regain control of the situation. "Okay, just relax."

Mr. Mime kept miming faster and faster, fully panicked.

"Round . . . Round house?" guessed Tim. "The source of the 'R' came from the Roundhouse?"

Mr. Mime pointed at Tim letting him know that he was correct, then collapsed.

"Nice work, kid," Detective Pikachu said. "Maybe there's a little detective in you after all."

Then, Tim accidentally dropped the imaginary match.

CHAPTER
10

Tim and Pikachu located the Roundhouse, which turned out to be some sort of underground club. Inside, music blared from a row of what looked like speakers up in the balcony—but on closer inspection, they were the ears of Loudred, which surrounded the club's DJ booth.

Down on the floor, Tim and Pikachu made their way through the crowd, which wrapped around a circular caged battle arena. A Pokémon battle was in full swing—Blastoise vs. Gengar. Gengar took a massive hit from Blastoise. Gengar crazily counterattacked Blastoise, who in turn responded equally wildly.

"I didn't know they had Pokémon battles in Ryme City," said Tim.

"They're not supposed to," said Pikachu. "Let's take a look around."

Sebastian, the battle announcer, surveyed the scene from the DJ booth. He wore a fur-lined coat over his bare chest, which showed off a tattoo of Charizard.

The light from Gengar's energy blasts illuminated a woman in a dark suit, wearing sunglasses. She spotted Tim and Pikachu, pulled out her phone, and texted: *The kid's here. And he's with the Pikachu.*

Tim and Pikachu made their way through the spectators as the battle continued.

"Okay, kid, so here's what we know," recapped Pikachu. "Harry traced the 'R' to here. Then, he frequents this joint because someone here knows something about something. We just need to find the someone . . . and the something."

Sebastian yelled out over the loudspeakers at Tim and Pikachu. He was staring down at them from the DJ booth. He descended down to the floor, and an entourage of fans fawned over him like he was a celebrity.

"Where's that Pikachu's partner?" Sebastian demanded.

"I think the someone just found us," Tim suggested to Pikachu.

Sebastian walked up to them menacingly, demanding to know who Tim was. Pikachu whispered to him, and Tim followed his advice reluctantly—telling Sebastian that he was Pikachu's new partner.

"Well, that Pikachu's Thunderbolt almost wrecked my prize Charizard the last time he was here. The scar's still fresh," Sebastian said, clearly as a challenge. His Charizard stepped into view. A lightning-shaped scar ran across its face and wing. It sneered at them both. Sebastian continued, "And you know what? He ruined my coat!"

"I'm so sorry," apologized Tim.

"Never mind the coat—where's his shirt?" Detective Pikachu said to Tim.

But Sebastian wasn't done ranting. "This is my place! And nobody comes into my place, and does that to my Pokémon. Or my coat."

"Look," Tim said, "I just want to know why his old partner was here. That's all."

"And I want a rematch," demanded Sebastian. "You give me my rematch, and I'll tell you everything you want to know."

"Tell him he's on!" Pikachu cried.

The LED wall display overhead was changed from

BLASTOISE VS. GENGAR to PIKACHU VS. CHARIZARD as they set up for the battle. The DJ took over announcing when Sebastian moved down to the battle arena to manage Charizard. "A new battle is unfolding: Pikachu versus Charizard. Rematch!"

Detective Pikachu stepped into the battle arena and passed his hat to Tim, who stood just outside the ring looking helpless. "Here, hold my hat. I'm about to rock this place," bragged Pikachu. "I'll just do a bit of light stretching. You never want to go into these things tight."

But Tim was more concerned about the upcoming battle than stretching. "What are you doing? What is your plan of attack?" he asked Pikachu.

"I don't operate according to plans, kid. I deal with things in the moment," Pikachu said a bit too confidently.

Across the arena, Sebastian opened his coat. It was loaded with dozens of vials—the very same glass vials of "R." He opened up one vial, exposing Charizard to the "R," then he opened another and another to intensify it. "You're going to win this time," he told Charizard.

"Obviously, I've dealt with this bozo before, so I'll just do it again," Pikachu boasted to Tim.

That all changed when Charizard burst into the arena ready to go nuclear. Then Pikachu began to panic. "Give me my hat back. That thing just chugged a year's worth of crazy juice!"

But it was too late. There was nothing that could be done. The cage was closed behind Pikachu and locked three times. Pikachu was stuck inside and had no choice but to battle.

"Hey, hey, hey, it's like you said, okay—you did it before," Tim said, trying to reassure Pikachu. "You've just gotta use your powers. You can use Quick Attack, Discharge, or Electro Ball. But we know that Volt Tackle is your best move, so start with that."

"First of all, when did you learn how to be a Pokémon Trainer?" Pikachu asked, a little surprised by Tim's knowledge. "And secondly, get me out of here!!"

The DJ announced the beginning of the battle as the LED screen changed to read BEGIN! Charizard banged its head against the ground, dug its feet into the ground, and then charged. Pikachu quickly dove clear.

"Whoa, whoa, whoa," Pikachu called out to Tim. "I forgot everything you said! I forget things! It's what I do! I have amnesia!"

"You need to go for a critical hit! Use Volt Tackle!" Tim coached from the sidelines. "Come on, come on, come on. You got it. You got it."

Detective Pikachu started to prepare for the attack. He

built his energy; his red cheeks started to vibrate, his face intensified, then his whole body strained . . . but nothing happened. It almost looked like Pikachu had to go to the bathroom.

"Hey, bud," said a worried Tim. "What are you doing?"

Pikachu cried, panicked. "It's not working! I forgot how to use my powers. But he didn't!"

Charizard rushed at Pikachu, who ran away as fast as its two little legs could carry him. *Wham!* Charizard's tail smacked Pikachu across the ring and against the cage. Pikachu was dazed.

"Taken out in one hit," the DJ announced to the crowd.

Sebastian celebrated from his corner. "Ah, Pikachu. Want to cry?!" he taunted.

Pikachu was cornered. Charizard was bearing down on him, and it looked like it was curtains for Pikachu. Tim watched in horror, unsure of what to do. Charizard opened its mouth wide as a storm of fire filled it. Pikachu closed its eyes, waiting for the end . . . but suddenly, Charizard lurched backward. Flames shot out of its mouth but missed their target. As the flames cleared, Pikachu saw that Tim was in the cage, too, trying to stomp out the fire on Charizard's tail.

"Are you crazy?!" cried Sebastian as the crowd booed furiously. "Get outta there!"

Then Charizard turned on Tim, about to attack. Pikachu ran up the back of Charizard, grabbed it by the eyelids, and pulled back on them with all his might. Charizard spun around wildly. Its tail connected with Tim's chest, and Tim grabbed on for dear life as he got dragged along. "AAAAAAHHHHH!" he screamed.

Charizard raced around the ring, piloted by Pikachu pulling on its eyelids. Tim eventually slammed into the cage wall.

Sebastian stepped into the arena. "What are you doing to my baby?" he cried.

"Get out of the way!" warned Pikachu.

Pikachu yanked hard. Charizard spun in place, sending Tim flying off its tail and into Sebastian, who fell to the ground. Sebastian's stash of "R" vials flew out of his coat and shattered on the floor. Purple gas spread into the crowd. All the Pokémon in the club started to inhale the gas.

"Uh-oh. That's not good!" Sebastian gasped.

It was complete mayhem after that. Loudred started to beatbox speed metal. The water tank below them shattered, spilling Magikarp all over the floor. The DJ dove off the balcony just as the Pokémon around him went wild, and all the humans in the club fled for the exits. Sebastian tried to run, too, but Tim held him down by his neck. For the first time, there was real rage in Tim's eyes. "Tell me what you know," he demanded.

"The guy you're looking for wanted to know the source of 'R,'" confessed Sebastian, who was totally taken aback by Tim's strength and anger. "It comes from the doctor. That's all I know. Now let me go!"

All of a sudden, Sebastian's eyes went wide. Directly behind Tim, Pikachu had just steered Charizard into the ceiling. *Smash!* Charizard got stuck in the lighting, and Pikachu had nowhere to go but down. Just as Pikachu was about to crash to the floor, Tim released Sebastian and dove to catch him.

"Nice catch, kid," Detective Pikachu cried. "Now let's get out of here!"

Just as Tim and Pikachu tried to make a run for it, Charizard blocked the exit doors and moved in to attack. But Pikachu had a plan—he raced across the floor, grabbed a Magikarp flapping spasmodically on the ground, and lifted it over his head.

"What are you doing? Magikarp is the worst," Tim said.

"Magikarp can evolve to Gyarados. All it needs is a little kick!" Pikachu assured Tim. Then he drop-kicked the

Magikarp across the club. "Water in the hole!" Pikachu yelled.

The Magikarp landed with a thud. The only problem was . . . nothing happened. There was a *ROAR* from Charizard as it gained on Pikachu and Tim. Just as they thought they were toast, the Magikarp stirred—and evolved into a massive Gyarados. The Charizard recoiled as the Gyarados opened its mouth. A geyser of water shot out, sending Tim, Pikachu, and the Charizard flying backward. *Whoosh!* The flood of water blasted them out the front doors of the Roundhouse, washing them on to the street. Pikachu and Tim finally slid to a stop, looked at each other, and began laughing hysterically. All the adrenaline had hit them hard. "Ha! I told you Magikarp weren't useless," Pikachu bragged to Tim.

But their celebration didn't last long. A few moments later, a swarm of police officers appeared above them and yelled, "You're under arrest!"

Tim and Pikachu didn't resist.

CHAPTER 11

A little while later, Detective Pikachu and Tim found themselves sitting in Lieutenant Yoshida's office in the Ryme City Police Department. "I thought you couldn't wait to get home," Yoshida said to Tim.

"Yeah, well, my plans changed because I found him," Tim began, pointing at Pikachu. "Harry's not dead. If his Pokémon partner is still alive, that means he is, too."

Yoshida sighed. "That is not proof, son."

"Tell him about the chemical 'R,'" suggested Pikachu.

"Give me a minute," Tim snapped at Pikachu.

Yoshida noticed Tim was acting strangely—was he having a conversation with Pikachu?

"Harry's last case had to do with those underground

battles," Tim began. "That's why I was there. There's a chemical—"

Yoshida interrupted him. "We ran an investigation. That case has blown over."

"Harry figured it out, and he's in trouble. You've got to reopen the investigation," Tim pleaded. "He's out there. I can feel it."

"In your jellies," added Pikachu. "Go ahead, say it!"

"I'm not going to say that," Tim shouted, growing increasingly frustrated that no one was taking him seriously. He took a deep breath. He could tell Yoshida was picking up on his odd behavior.

"I can feel it, Lieutenant," Tim said. "In my . . . bones."

"Not as good." Detective Pikachu shook his head.

"Stop!" Tim finally yelled at Pikachu. Then he turned back toward Yoshida, who was giving him a strange look.

"Oh, yeah, and I can understand Pikachu," he admitted. "Like, word-perfect. So . . ."

That last detail didn't help Tim's case. Yoshida was now very concerned about Tim. "It's difficult coping with loss," Yoshida said calmly, so he didn't upset Tim any further. "Denial can be a powerful thing . . ."

"No, I'm not in denial! I'm right! I know it!" Tim protested. "He's out there."

With a heavy heart, Yoshida turned on his TV. "I never wanted to show you this, but I think it's important you see it."

Grainy CCTV footage of Harry's car crash played on the screen. Tim watched as the car careened off the bridge and exploded.

"No one could survive a crash like that." Yoshida explained, not without sympathy. "Not even your dad. He's gone, Tim."

CHAPTER 12

It was late. The streets were all but empty. Tim and Pikachu sat quietly on a bench outside the police department. Finally, Tim broke the silence. "I should've gotten on that train."

"What's that, kid?" asked Pikachu.

"After my mom died, my dad and I drifted apart." Tim admitted. "He moved here and poured himself into his work. Eventually, he tried to get me to come live with him, but I wouldn't go. I didn't think he cared. I guess I just got used to him not being around and I couldn't forgive him for it." Tim looked straight down at his lap. "When I got here, I realized that he did care. But I didn't know, because I never gave him the chance. And now it's too late. I really, really wish I got on that train."

"Listen, kid, um . . . Look, I may not have memories,

but I know this much . . . It wasn't your fault. It wasn't anybody's fault," Detective Pikachu said gently. "And I'm sure that if your dad was here, he would hug you so hard your bones would pop, and he'd tell you he's sorry for everything. He'd be so proud of you, kid."

Tears pooled in Tim's eyes. "I haven't been really nice to you," he said apologetically.

"No, you have really haven't," Pikachu agreed.

Tim reached into his pocket and pulled out Pikachu's detective hat. He put it on Pikachu's head, adjusting it to a snug fit. "Well, we still have one mystery to solve," he said.

"What?" asked Pikachu.

"Yours!" exclaimed Tim. "Let's go find out who did this to you. Get your memory back."

Pikachu smiled, clearly touched. "I'd like that. I'd like that very much."

Just then, an enormous black SUV ominously pulled up to the curb right in front of them.

"Well, that's a bad guy car," Pikachu said drily.

The passenger door opened, revealing the woman in the dark suit and sunglasses who'd seen them at the Roundhouse. She gestured for them to come with her. Tim and Pikachu glanced at each other, and then reluctantly got into the car.

They were taken to the CNM building. The whole time,

the woman in the dark suit didn't say a word, even when they went inside. She just stared at them through her sunglasses as they rode a glass elevator all the way up to the penthouse. When the elevator doors opened, Tim and Pikachu were ushered into a massive room. A lone figure sat in the darkness.

"Thank you, Ms. Norman," the hidden figure said. His curt tone served as a dismissal, and she nodded and exited.

Tim and Pikachu suddenly noticed an Eevee sniffing a Fire Stone in a tray on the desk.

"Please come in. Magnificent creatures, aren't they?" said the mystery man.

All of a sudden, the Eevee evolved into Flareon in a beautiful flash. Tim and Pikachu were a bit taken aback.

"You don't see that every day!" Detective Pikachu said.

The hidden figure continued speaking. "Imagine being able to evolve into the best possible version of yourself. That greatness inside you just waiting to be awoken." The Flareon walked over to him as he moved into the light. It was a man in a high-tech wheelchair: Howard Clifford. "Hello, Tim," he said, smiling. "I see you've partnered with Harry's Pikachu."

"You knew Harry?" asked Tim. He and Pikachu gave each other a look.

"The case Harry was working on—it was for me," explained Howard.

"That's a twist. That's very twisty," remarked Pikachu.

Howard held up a vial of "R." "This compound threatens everything I've built."

"He knows about the 'R'!" cried Pikachu to Tim. "How does he know about the 'R'?"

Howard continued explaining to Tim. "I hired Harry to trace it to its source. Imagine my shock when the answer turned out to be my own son. I devoted my life to perfecting the partnership between Pokémon and humans—a partnership where Pokémon bring out the best in us. In doing so, I'm afraid I neglected my responsibilities as a parent." Howard shook his head sadly as he approached an ancient sculpture depicting a human and a Pokémon holding hands. "Roger resents Pokémon. I think he's lived in my shadow for so long that he actually wants to destroy my legacy."

"But, Mr. Clifford, how could you let him do that?" asked Tim.

"Ever since my illness put me in this chair, Roger has taken over more and more of the company. He controls the board. He also controls the police, the politicians, and he owns the press. Harry is the only one I can trust. That is why you need to find him."

Tim shook his head. "You haven't heard? Harry's dead."

"Oh, no, Tim," Howard said. "Your father is alive."

Tim found out his dad, Detective Harry Goodman, had died in a car crash.

WELCOME TO
RYME CITY
WHERE PEOPLE AND POKÉMON COEXIST

RYME CITY COUNCIL

He traveled to Ryme City, where his dad lived—a place where people and Pokémon live together in harmony.

Tim made his way to his dad's apartment, where he found a bedroom his dad had set up for him to stay in.

Then he heard a noise in the living room. Was someone there?

To his surprise, a Pikachu in a detective hat revealed himself!

Even crazier: Tim and Detective Pikachu could understand each other!

Detective Pikachu had been Harry's Pokémon partner—
and even though he had amnesia, he was convinced
that Harry was still alive.

Tim was skeptical, but in the marketplace and the Hi-Hat Cafe, Detective Pikachu tried to convince him that they should work together.

Tim finally agreed. He and Detective Pikachu began to track down clues about what happened to Harry.

They teamed up with a junior reporter named Lucy and her Psyduck partner.

Their search took them on a wild adventure, from an interrogation in a seedy warehouse . . .

to a secret battle arena . . .

to a mysterious laboratory.

Could they find out the truth—and save the day—
before it was too late?

Howard pressed a button. Instantly the walls dissolved and in their place a car sped toward them and crashed. Tim and Pikachu dove for the floor, but soon realized there was no flying debris in the room.

"This is advanced holographic imaging," Howard explained. "Since being confined to this chair, I've invested in ways of bringing the world to me."

Tim and Pikachu looked up and discovered that they were now standing a bit farther away from the crashed car, on a calm country road outside the city, still at night.

Howard continued, "This was re-created from the police footage. It allows us to see things that they cannot. Or don't want us to see."

Tim walked around the crashed car, and discovered Harry. He was alive—but lying facedown beside the car, barely moving. A few yards away, a hologram of Pikachu climbed out of the car. Detective Pikachu studied its holographic self. "It's me. I was with Harry in the crash."

"He needs my help," Tim said. He reached down to help his father, but his hand went right through the hologram. Tim looked up at Howard. "If Harry is alive, why didn't they find him?"

Suddenly, Mewtwo entered the hologram scene, hovering over Harry. Detective Pikachu stepped back, awestruck, and circled the hologram of the infamous Legendary Pokémon.

"What is that?" asked Tim.

"Mewtwo. A man-made abomination created in a laboratory using DNA from the fossil remains of the ancient Mew," explained Howard.

"I can't believe it," said Pikachu to Tim. "If that thing came from Mew, we're looking at the most powerful Pokémon in the world."

Mewtwo descended over Harry and with telekinetic power, lifted Harry's body into the air. The Pikachu in the hologram said something to Mewtwo. Then, Mewtwo put out its hand and washed Pikachu with purple energy. Pikachu dropped unconscious.

"That's it. That's what happened to me," Pikachu said to Tim. He was excited—he'd finally found out what had happened to him! "Mewtwo wiped my memory. But why?"

Suddenly, the car in the hologram sparked and erupted into a massive explosion. The hologram ended and the room returned to normal.

"Wait, wait, wait, wait!" shouted Tim. "Where did it take him?"

"That's for you to solve now," said Howard. "Find Mewtwo, and you will find your father."

CHAPTER 13

Tim and Detective Pikachu couldn't believe what they had just learned. "Where are we going?" asked Pikachu as they headed out of the CNM building into the streets of Ryme City.

"I don't know. I'm just going," said Tim. "You've gotta tell me where. You're the detective."

"Okay," Pikachu said, taking charge. "If Roger Clifford is the key to all of this . . ."

"Then we need someone who has access to him," Tim finished.

"And we both know who that is, lover boy," added Detective Pikachu.

A short while later, Tim and Pikachu sat in a booth at the Hi-Hat Cafe, drinking coffee. They were waiting for someone, and that someone was Lucy.

Lucy soon entered the cafe wearing huge sunglasses, a headscarf, and a trench coat. "There she is," said Tim. She was clearly trying to be covert as she made her way over to them, but she was failing miserably.

"What's with the sunglasses?" Pikachu asked. "Can she see us? I don't think she can see us."

Tim started to stand. "Hey, thanks for coming . . ."

"Don't talk to me," Lucy said sternly, and shoved Tim back down into his seat. She sat down in the next booth so she was back-to-back with Tim, then picked up a menu and pretended to read it.

Tim was feeling a bit confused about the situation, but he didn't want to make Lucy mad. He asked tentatively, "Okay. What happens now?"

"Just act casual," Lucy whispered back. Tim turned to talk to her, but she scolded him again. "But don't look at me!"

Tim turned back around, terrified to make another mistake. "There's nothing really casual about this," he said.

"Look at this," Lucy instructed. She reached into her trench coat and pulled out a thick binder of folders. She tried to stealthily pass it backward to Tim over her shoulder . . . but all the papers ended up spilling out all over the floor, making a huge mess and causing a minor scene in the cafe.

Tim immediately got down on the floor to help gather the papers. Just as he was saying, "Sorry, that was my faul—" he and Lucy bumped heads, which caused them both to yelp, and knocked off Lucy's sunglasses. Everyone was looking at them.

"Oh, ah—this is working out great," said Pikachu sarcastically. "Why don't you just have her sit over here?"

Tim followed Pikachu's advice and invited Lucy to sit with them. Thankfully, Lucy agreed, and joined them in the booth after she finished gathering up the files.

"I got access to Roger's computer," she said.

"Oh, wow!" said Tim, totally impressed. "How did you do that?"

"I spilled cappuccino in his lap," said Lucy. Even Pikachu was impressed at that! Lucy continued, "So I searched through all his records. I targeted the property rights in the region and I cross-checked that with city records for any Clifford financed businesses until I found it. May I present PCL—a Pokémon genetic research facility."

Lucy slid a photo of the facility across the table. "But that's not all. Last week, PCL had an accident and had to shut down their entire facility. That was the same night

Harry Goodman went missing. No one knows what happened—total media blackout. What does it all mean? I don't know!"

"She's good," observed Pikachu, tapping Tim on the shoulder.

Lucy looked at Tim eagerly. "This is very exciting—are you excited?"

Tim nodded and said, "So there's a cover-up . . . but what are they covering up?"

Lucy dangled her car keys. "What do you say we go find out?"

Tim and Pikachu didn't have to be asked twice.

The next morning, they were all packed into Lucy's car, driving out of Ryme City and across rolling fields up into the mountains. Tim sat in the passenger seat, staring at Lucy—totally smitten with her. In the back seat, in booster seats, were Pikachu and Psyduck.

Lucy caught Tim staring at her and demanded to know what was up. "Nothing!" Tim said hastily. "Um, I was actually wondering who this was?" He pulled a newspaper clipping with a photo of Dr. Laurent out of a folder full of research.

Lucy glanced at it. "That's PCL's chief scientist, Dr. Ann Laurent. She lost her university grant over experimentation on Pokémon because she was trying to control their minds. She's essentially a neurologist for Pokémon."

"I bet this was the doctor that Shirtless was talking about," suggested Pikachu, referring to Sebastian from the club. He shifted in his seat, and added, "Maybe she could weigh into the long-term psychological effects of being strapped into a baby seat."

Tim ignored him.

"This is it," Lucy announced as she slowed the car. In front of them was a large chain-link fence, with signs that read DANGER and VIRULENT BIOLOGICAL AGENTS IN THIS AREA: STAY OUT! Behind the fence was a field and several large buildings in the distance with no lights on or apparent human activity. It was a total ghost town.

They all exited the car, and Lucy put Psyduck in a baby carrier.

"Look at the signs. Must've been a really bad accident," observed Lucy.

"That's what they want you to believe," said Pikachu as he and Tim headed over to the signs to investigate. "Whoever staged this did an excellent job. Those signs are the perfect scarecrows for suckers."

"Yeah, well, they're working on me," admitted Tim.

"Kid, this dame's looking for danger. You wanna win

her over? You gotta lead her straight to it," coached Pikachu.

"Okay, okay," said Tim, annoyed. "First of all, women don't like to be called 'dame.' Second, women appreciate calm, level-headed, and responsible decision-making—what is she doing?"

Out of the corner of his eye, Tim saw Lucy using wire cutters to make a hole in the fence. He ran over to her. "Hey, hey, hey, hey! Lucy! What are you doing?"

"I'm cutting the fence so that we can slip through," Lucy responded in a tone that implied "*Obviously*."

Once they all scooted through the hole in the fence, they scurried across the field toward the lab. The doors were locked, but Lucy figured out a way to break in through a vent in the roof. Luckily, the building was only one story.

She dropped down gracefully in a quiet corridor of the building. Psyduck jumped through next, and Lucy caught it. Then Tim dropped down, landing much more awkwardly than Lucy, followed by Detective Pikachu, who made a soft landing on Tim's shoulder. Pikachu was about to jump down from his shoulder when Tim said, "You can stay up there." Pikachu smiled.

Emergency lights flickered and cast strange shadows along the hallway. The lab's rooms were all walled off by thick glass, like some sort of high-tech zoo.

"I may have amnesia, but I'm pretty sure breaking in here is the worst idea anyone's ever had," said Pikachu.

Lucy approached one of the windows and Tim followed. They both leaned in close, trying to see what was inside. "What is that?" asked Lucy.

"I'm not sure . . ." said Tim, a little concerned about what they were getting into.

Splat! A Greninja suddenly hit the glass, startling Tim. Now he could see that four Greninja in total were inside the room.

"It's Greninja," noted Lucy. "But they don't look right."

Tim agreed. They all looked slightly altered from how Greninja usually appeared. It was almost as if they had been . . . weaponized.

Pikachu found a medical chart on the wall and thumbed through it. He read aloud: "Test twenty-two: Power Enhancement."

"They were experimenting on them," said Tim, breathing out slowly. That was terrible. He stared through the glass, feeling bad for the Greninja. Lucy took photographs, documenting everything.

"Why?" wondered Pikachu. "If Roger Clifford's behind this, what's he doing experimenting on Pokémon?"

They continued on to another chamber. When they peered through the glass, they could see a small greenhouse lined with a clear plastic tarp. But it wasn't just a regular greenhouse—suddenly, two bonsai trees moved. They realized that the trees were actually growing from the backs of Torterra.

"A Torterra garden?" asked Lucy.

Tim checked the medical chart by the window and read the title aloud: "Test thirty-three: Growth Enhancement." A strange symbol was watermarked on the pages.

"They look normal size to me," said Lucy, puzzled. "It's like they're trying to manipulate Pokémon Evolution."

"Is that even possible?" asked Tim.

"I don't know," said Lucy, trying to take pictures of every single detail. "I need to document all of this, though."

Meanwhile, in the back of an SUV, Roger Clifford sat and watched security footage of Tim, Pikachu, Lucy, and Psyduck . . .

Back in the lab building, Tim and Detective Pikachu approached the main laboratory. The doors had been blasted open as if by some sort of prior explosion, and the lights flickered eerily. Tim and Pikachu exchanged a look.

They headed into the destroyed lab. Shattered glass

and melted metal was everywhere. Equipment was overturned and in disarray. In the center of the lab was a giant sphere, but its glass face had been blasted to pieces.

"Whoa!" said Tim, a little shaken. "What happened here?"

"Bad stuff," said Pikachu. "Really bad stuff!"

"Still think this was staged?" Tim asked Pikachu. He shook his head. This was too much destruction. Something had really happened here.

Meanwhile, Lucy was still back by the Greninja chamber, snapping photo after photo. Psyduck looked around nervously. Lucy was so preoccupied with capturing every detail, she was unaware that the vents had opened and were releasing "R" into the Greninja chamber. But Psyduck noticed, and began to panic.

The Greninja breathed in the purple gas and began to go wild. And then . . . the glass wall retracted, opening the chamber.

Psyduck tried to warn Lucy. *"Psyduck, psyduck, psyduuuuck!"* But Lucy still hadn't noticed. As she continued to record footage of the room, a Greninja hand gripped the chamber opening.

Back in the destroyed main lab, Pikachu found a blinking

light. "Kid, hey. Over here. It says 'Dr. Laurent's station.'"

Tim stepped up to the computer terminal. It was still at least semi-functional—the cursor blinked on the screen. "Looks like it's still working," Tim said. He touched the screen and its interface lit up.

At the same time, a security camera in the back corner of the room turned on and a red light started to flash. Unaware, Tim and Pikachu studied the active computer screen.

"Looks like most of the files are corrupted," said Tim. He pushed a button. *Whoosh!* All the lights suddenly turned on.

"Uh-oh. Another one of those holograms," said Pikachu.

In a blink of an eye, they saw the lab pieced back together. Tim and Pikachu were inside a holograph record-ing of the past. Tim jolted—someone was standing right next to him. It was Dr. Ann Laurent, the head scientist, recording her findings.

She spoke. "Day forty-two: After much trial and error we perfected a stable method to extract Mewtwo's DNA." Then she walked right through Tim and stepped up to the spherical containment chamber. Tim followed her to it and peered inside. Mewtwo was trapped there, frozen.

"It's Mewtwo. No, wait . . . wait, Mewtwo came from this place?" asked Pikachu.

There was a glitch and the hologram jumped forward in time. "Day sixty: Clinical trials proven successful," said Dr. Laurent.

The hologram flashed ahead again. Tim spun around and found Dr. Laurent by a wall. Several thin tubes attached to the containment chamber led across the lab to a machine that was filling up vials of "R."

"The inhalant results in confusion and a total loss of free will, which in turn makes the Pokémon go wild," Dr. Laurent noted. "We have designated the chemical as serum 'R.'" She held up a vial of "R" and stared at it in wonder.

Tim couldn't believe it. "They used Mewtwo to make 'R'!"

"And they were testing it at the battles," added Pikachu.

The hologram flashed ahead again. Dr. Laurent was now on the opposite side of the lab. Tim approached her hologram as she grabbed some complicated-looking headgear.

"Day sixty-eight: The neural link is operational," stated Dr. Laurent.

All of a sudden, warning notifications flashed and beeped on Laurent's console. An automated voice sounded an alert: "Condition red." Dr. Laurent panicked. "No, no, no. We're losing power to the containment cha—"

Dr. Laurent spun around and caught Mewtwo eyeing her from within the containment chamber. Mewtwo was glowing with purple energy, looking angry. Then suddenly, it burst free from the chamber. Dr. Laurent screamed as an explosion of purple energy washed over the entire lab, causing chaos.

And then, the holographic recording abruptly ended. Tim and Pikachu were once again in the present day—in the hauntingly quiet lab ruins.

Tim stepped up to the console and scanned the files. "That must've been how Mewtwo escaped."

"Now we're getting somewhere," said Pikachu, itching to solve the case once and for all.

"What did that thing want with Harry?" Tim wondered. He thought back to the first hologram they watched in Howard's office—of Mewtwo carrying Harry off to who-knows-where.

"Good question, kid. I'll try and take us back to the beginning." Pikachu scanned the files and chose the first file in the log. The room was transformed with another hologram into a much earlier version of the lab—just as it was all being initially set up. The containment chamber was empty. Its glass door was open, and scientists were preparing its interior. The floor was littered with equipment that was still in boxes. Dr. Laurent was recording her very first log. In contrast to her tired demeanor in the previous hologram, here Laurent appeared fresh and enthusiastic about getting to work.

"Day one: The lab is almost fully operational," she said. "All that remains now is to capture the most powerful Pokémon known to mankind: Mewtwo. It escaped nearly twenty years ago from the Kanto region. Fortunately, our benefactors hired a specialist for the task. Good luck, Detective Goodman!"

Tim and Pikachu were shocked to hear Harry's name—and then to see Harry nodding and heading for the exit. Tim reached out as Harry's hologram walked by him. But just as before, his hand went right through Harry.

"That's why Mewtwo took Harry!" concluded Pikachu. "It was revenge for being captured."

"That doesn't make any sense," argued Tim. "Harry would have never been a part of this."

"I want to believe that, kid. But we gotta be honest here—you haven't seen him in years, and I've got amnesia. Neither of us can say for sure what Harry would or wouldn't do."

"We gotta get back to the city," Tim said.

Tim and Pikachu ran back into the empty corridor. "Lucy! Lucy! We've got to—"

They stood at the end of the long dark hallway where Lucy had been just a few moments ago. It was quiet—too quiet. There was no Lucy. Then they realized the Greninja pods were open.

"Lucy? . . . Lucy?" Tim called out, worried.

They heard a splat behind them, and walked toward it. A drop of slime was puddled on the floor. Something was wrong. "That was not there before, kid," Pikachu said.

Another drop of slime landed on Pikachu's hat. He took it off and looked at it. "Ewww!"

Tim and Pikachu slowly looked up, and saw . . . a Greninja stuck to the ceiling, with its tongue wrapped tight around Lucy and Psyduck. Lucy's eyes were bugged out, panicked and pleading. And then quickly annoyed—why weren't they doing anything?! Her eyes shifted to the corner, signaling to Tim to look.

There was another Greninja. Its tongue was just flying

down toward them when Tim dove out of the way and Pikachu dropped to the floor. Tim was lying low against a wall, and Pikachu noticed an emergency fire alarm just above him.

"Kid, fire alarm!" yelled Pikachu.

Tim pulled the lever. Fire suppressant erupted out of the ceiling, alarms blared, and red lights swirled. The distraction caused the Grininja to release Lucy and Psyduck, who fell to the ground. Tim helped them up, and the four of them darted through the hallway, trying to avoid the fire suppressant and get out of the building.

"Come, on, let's go, let's go, let's go!" Tim shouted.

But as they reached a corner up ahead, two more Greninja appeared. They were trapped!

"Go back the other way!" called Tim, and they raced back in the direction they'd just come from.

The fire suppressant had stopped and two Greninja were headed their way. They backed off toward a window and got low to the ground as a storm of Greninja Shuriken—throwing stars made of compressed water— whizzed past them. The Shuriken stuck into the wall all around them. One cracked the glass wall of the Torterra Garden.

"Get down," warned Lucy. She quickly grabbed a piece

of equipment nearby, lifted it, and hurled it into the cracked glass of the Torterra Garden. The glass shattered everywhere! Tim, Detective Pikachu, and Lucy carrying Psyduck leaped through the now-open window into the Torterra Garden.

Once inside, they quickly hopscotched across the backs of the Torterra until they reached the other side of the room, where they ripped aside the clear plastic tarp—and found themselves in a forest.

Without questioning this turn of events, they ran for their lives—racing through the trees and working their way deeper and deeper into the forest. Behind them they could hear the rustling of trees—which meant the Greninja were leaving the lab and making their way into the forest as well.

Psyduck realized this first and started twitching and freaking out. *"Psyduck! Psyduck! Psyduck! Psyyyduck!"*

"It's okay. It's okay," Lucy repeated, trying to soothe Psyduck. "Everything's fine."

"He's going to blow his deck, kid," warned Pikachu.

"It's okay, Psyduck! It's okay," said Tim, trying to help get the situation under control.

"This is no time for your stupid headaches!" Pikachu said. Then he had a thought. "No, no, no, wait. Wait. This is the perfect time to get a headache! Get a headache now—you're neurotic! Do it! Do it! Do it!"

Greninja smashed through the forest and ran along the treetops. A deluge of Shuriken rained down. There was no escape. They were about to be sliced to pieces!

Suddenly . . . *"PSYDUUUUUUCK!"*

Boooom! Psyduck got a headache. A blue energy burst of psionic brain waves erupted from Psyduck. The shockwaves repelled the Greninja and their Shuriken, sending them flying out of sight. Lucy, Tim, and Pikachu hit the floor and covered their heads. A few moments later, everything settled down.

"Good job, Psyduck," Detective Pikachu said, relieved. "Where's my hat?"

Tim sat holding his head, and slowly opened his eyes. He noticed a nearby fern—water droplets had begun to shake off of it. "Something's wrong," he said.

Suddenly, the ground began to shake and rumble. They weren't out of the woods yet.

"Is this really happening?" Lucy cried. Everyone turned to see trees in the distance rising up, as the forest seemed to be folding in on itself.

"Don't worry," comforted Pikachu. "Psyduck's psionic waves are causing hallucinations. None of this is real."

But then there was an explosion. The folding forest of trees connected and smashed into one another. A huge tree trunk slammed down right next to them. Pikachu cried out, "Nope, all of this is real. Run!"

They all took off running as the forest folded in toward them. There was an avalanche of rock, dirt, and trees at their heels. Then the forest turned on its side, the ground tilting 180 degrees. They went from running on a flat surface to running uphill to climbing completely vertically. They grabbed on to vines and hung like they were on the side of a cliff. Boulders began to dislodge above them and careen down toward them.

They let go, and slid at full speed down the side of the forest . . . until a horizontal tree trunk caught them. Pikachu dangled from the side of the trunk, and Tim pulled him up onto his shoulder.

Crash! Trees collided with a roar. They looked back and saw two walls of the forest heading toward them, zippering together, closer and closer. They jumped from tree to tree to try to avoid being squashed, and finally dropped down to some level ground. For a moment, things were quiet and still.

"I officially hate this forest," declared Pikachu.

But they didn't have much time to relax. Suddenly, the

ground split right in half like a high-speed earthquake. Tim and Pikachu were on the opposite sides of a monster ravine from Lucy and Psyduck.

Lucy ran along the newly formed ledge. She tried to keep up with the mountainside Tim was standing on. Pikachu hopped on Tim's shoulders and noticed something in the distance. "Kid, we gotta do something," he said. "We gotta do it now."

Tim turned around. The forest behind them was giving way! An avalanche of rocks and trees was barreling toward them. Lucy was still safe on the other side of the ravine. Tim made a decision. "I gotta jump for it," he said, sprinting along the ledge.

"You're not going to make it," cried Lucy.

But Tim was determined. There was no other choice. He backed up a few steps and started to run. With all his might, Tim flew through the air, flailing his arms. Pikachu held on tight to Tim's jacket collar with one hand and to his own hat with the other. The ledge approached fast and furiously, and Tim slammed into it—he just about made it. But then he slipped, and started to slide down the cliff face.

Just in time, Lucy grabbed his arm as tight as she could, and managed to pull him to safety. They both collapsed together on the ledge catching their breath.

Pikachu shook his head. "I thought I was gonna . . . I—I—Eyeball!"

"Eyeball!" Tim repeated, terrified. The boulder next to them had opened—and they were staring at an enormous eyeball.

"Oh, I get it! I get it now! This isn't a forest at all!" screamed Pikachu. "*This* is the Torterra Garden!" They hadn't been in a forest—they were on a humongous, genetically enhanced Torterra. And what they had just experienced was not a forest turning in on itself, but dozens of these enormous Torterra walking side by side.

Then, everything started shaking—the giant Torterra seemed to be trying to shake the forest off its back. Huge rocks tumbled everywhere, and there was nothing to hold on to. One of the rocks hit Pikachu, knocking him out. And then the section of forest they were standing on broke free and slid off the Torterra's back, and into a lake. *Splash!*

Tim carried Pikachu to the shore.

"He's hurt," Tim called out to Lucy, and he gently laid Pikachu down on the ground.

"Is he okay?" asked Lucy as Pikachu's eyes fluttered open briefly.

"I'm in bad shape, kid," Pikachu confided to Tim.

"I'm here, partner," Tim promised him. "I'm here."

"Did you just call me 'partner'?" asked a surprised Pikachu.

"Yeah, of course," said Tim. "You're my partner."

"Yeah, that's right . . . you got my back," Pikachu murmured as he closed his eyes and passed out.

"Hey, hey, bud. Hey, Pikachu. Pikachu! No . . ." Tim pleaded. He had to help Pikachu!

Just then, Tim noticed a Bulbasaur staring at them from the forest's edge. "Hey, Bulbasaur! Help! Please!" begged Tim.

"He doesn't know what you're saying," said Lucy.

"But he knows what I'm feeling," explained Tim. He turned once again to the Bulbasaur. "I need to get Pikachu to a healer Pokémon. Please. I'm begging you. I don't want to lose him, too."

The Bulbasaur peered up at Tim and made eye contact. It tilted its head. Then it wandered back into the forest.

Tim hung his head, broken and defeated. The Bulbasaur was gone. Pikachu lay lifelessly in his arms.

"*Psyduck!*" sounded Psyduck.

"Tim, look!" cried Lucy.

Tim looked up to see that the Bulbasaur had reappeared—and was leading a small herd of other

Bulbasaur out of the forest. They had come to help Pikachu! They motioned for Tim to come along with them, and he carefully picked up Pikachu and followed. Lucy tried to go with them, but the Bulbasaur created a wall of vines and blocked her path. Tim and Lucy exchanged a look. In the end, Lucy backed off, respecting the Pokémon's wishes.

"I'll meet you at the car," Lucy said to Tim.

Tim nodded and followed the Bulbasaur, keeping a worried eye on Pikachu while he walked. As they made their way through the woods, more and more Bulbasaur joined them. In the dusk, mushrooms in the ground began to move and glow—and soon pulled themselves out of the ground, revealing that they were actually Morelull. The forest took on an almost magical feel as the Morelull lit a path for the Bulbasaur to follow. Feeling a bit renewed with hope, Tim took Pikachu's limp hand in his and whispered to him. "You're going to be okay, partner."

The Bulbasaur led Tim and Pikachu deeper and deeper into the forest. Soon they entered a ravine that was clearly an ancient, mystical place. The Bulbasaur retreated into the forest with the Morelull, leaving Tim and Pikachu all alone.

"Hey! Wait—where you going?" Tim called out to the Bulbasaur. "What am I supposed to do?"

Just as Tim was about to give up all hope, he heard an ethereal voice that sounded like it was in his head. *"I've been waiting for you,"* it called out.

From out of nowhere, a purple light descended upon Tim and Pikachu. Tim turned to find Mewtwo hovering above them, pulsing with its signature purple energy. Tim took a step back, terrified. Mewtwo descended slowly, looking from Tim to Pikachu. Then, Mewtwo held out its hand, extending its purple energy over Pikachu's body.

"No, no, no, wait!" Tim cried. Was Mewtwo attacking them?

But then Tim could scarcely believe his eyes. The purple energy absorbed into Pikachu's body, and he rolled over. As Mewtwo withdrew the energy, Pikachu jolted awake. He was as good as new!

"Where am I?" he asked.

"You're okay!" Tim exclaimed, absolutely thrilled to have Pikachu back.

"Yeah! I'm . . . Somehow I'm fine," said Detective Pikachu, puzzled.

Mewtwo turned to Pikachu and spoke. *"You've brought the son to me, as agreed."*

When Pikachu heard Mewtwo and turned to see it for the first time, his eyes completely bugged out. Pikachu jumped up and stood protectively in front of a very confused-looking Tim.

"What is he talking about?" Tim asked.

"I don't know, kid," admitted Pikachu. "I'm as lost as you are."

Tim spun on Mewtwo, enraged. "Where's my father?!" He demanded. "What did you do with him?!"

Whoosh! Mewtwo hit them both with a blast of purple energy, warping them into a collection of memories.

In the first memory, they saw Pikachu outside the PCL lab at night. Pikachu was sabotaging the PCL lab power generator with his electric powers. An automatic voice could be heard announcing an alert, and then Mewtwo burst free from the lab.

The second memory flashed forward to just before Harry's car accident. Harry's car sped down the street. A Greninja threw a Shuriken that blew out a tire, and the car swerved off the bridge. Pikachu was thrown clear of the car. Then Pikachu looked up and saw Mewtwo hovering above. They seemed to have a conversation. Then Mewtwo told Pikachu, *"You've done well. Humanity is evil. I have always believed Pokémon must take care of our own."*

The memories came to a sudden end, and Tim and

Detective Pikachu snapped back to reality. Mewtwo spoke to Pikachu again, *"You led them to me."*

Suddenly, Mewtwo cried out. *"No!"*

Four capture drones appeared over the ridge, and soon ensnared Mewtwo with powerful technology. They forced Mewtwo higher and higher into the air.

"No!" Mewtwo twisted and struggled, but could not get free.

Soon, Tim and Detective Pikachu noticed a human appear atop the ravine—Roger Clifford, in his big, ugly designer sunglasses. He grinned at the scene unfolding in the air, then caught Detective Pikachu's eye, as if to say, "Thanks for your help."

Tim glanced at Detective Pikachu—he looked shaken.

Mewtwo was soon fully trapped and loaded into a truck waiting nearby. Roger supervised the operation, then got in the truck and drove away.

As they headed back to the lab, Tim was all fired up. But Pikachu was still shell-shocked from his recent near-death experience and from a horrible growing suspicion.

Tim stepped through the hole in the fence, and called back to Pikachu, "We need to talk about this." Then he realized Pikachu had stopped following him.

"You have to go on without me," Pikachu said.

"What are you saying?" asked Tim, in disbelief. "Roger has Mewtwo, and Mewtwo has my father. We're running out of time. We have a case to solve!"

"We already solved it," declared Pikachu. "I know who I am now. I'm the guy who betrayed Harry."

"We don't know that," insisted Tim.

Pikachu disagreed. "We both saw it. I betrayed your father, which means I could betray you, too."

"You wouldn't do that," Tim said. "I don't care what I saw. I know who you are."

"How do you know?" demanded Pikachu.

"Because . . . I can feel it in my jellies," said Tim, throwing Pikachu's words back at him.

"I made that up! There's no jellies! There's no me!" Pikachu said. "You're better off on your own."

"C'mon, Pikachu," pleaded Tim. "I need you. Please."

Tim took a step toward Pikachu. Pikachu's cheeks sparked, and his body started to crackle. "You have to stay away. It's for your own good," Pikachu warned with tears in his eyes.

"No!" Tim refused. "I'm not letting you go!"

A sudden electric charge burst from Pikachu and

struck Tim, knocking him back down to the ground. "Ah!" Tim cried out in pain.

Tim and Pikachu locked eyes. They were both alarmed by what had just happened. But for Pikachu, it was confirmation of his worst fears. "You see, I can't help it. I hurt the people who need me. That's who I am. I'm sorry," he said, and ran into the woods.

As Tim watched Pikachu leave him behind, Lucy arrived on the scene with Psyduck waddling next to her. She quickly helped Tim to his feet. "What happened?" Lucy wanted to know. "Is Pikachu okay?"

"No. He's not. Let's go. We've got to get back to the city," Tim announced, feeling slightly defeated. But he knew they had to continue on with their investigation no matter what.

Pikachu continued to retreat into the forest. He looked back once and watched Tim get into the car with Lucy. Pikachu hung his head low as the others drove away.

CHAPTER
14

Back in Ryme City, the citizens—both human and Pokémon—were beginning to gather for the big celebratory parade near the CNM building. In front of the building, giant Pokémon balloons were being inflated for the parade.

A giant TV screen showed a newscaster discussing the day's upcoming event. "The tenth anniversary Ryme City Pokémon parade is set to begin this afternoon. The whole city is converging on downtown to watch today's festivities."

Lucy's tiny, mud-covered car pulled up to CNM. As she put it into park, she turned to speak to Tim. "I don't know what happened between you and Pikachu, but we need to strategize—"

Tim hopped out of the car without replying. He started walking toward Clifford Tower.

Lucy quickly got out of the car and ran up to him. "Wait! Where are you going? We need to tell the public what we found out. Tim, this is breaking news!"

Tim stopped momentarily and turned to Lucy. "No. You should break the news. I'm going to talk to Howard."

And with that, Tim took off again. Feeling frustrated, Lucy called after him, "How am I supposed to break the news when the guy who runs the news IS the breaking news?!"

But Tim didn't stop again, and all Lucy could do was watch him walk away. Then she caught sight of a reporter she knew from work, Cynthia McMaster, who was about to broadcast live. Lucy instructed Psyduck to remain inside her car. Then she hustled over to the newscaster.

"Mrs. McMaster. Hi, it's Lucy Stevens, the intern at CNM. Yeah, um . . . I have a story that's really important that the people need to hear, and I was really hoping you could help me tell it. I just need—"

But the newscaster didn't pay any attention to what Lucy had just said. Instead she asked Lucy to fetch a coffee for her, tossed her red blazer at Lucy for safekeeping, and strolled off.

That's when Lucy noticed that Cynthia's press credentials were attached to the blazer. "You got it, Cynthia," Lucy responded as she unzipped her own jacket and took it off.

CHAPTER
15

Meanwhile, Detective Pikachu was still outside the city limits. He sang and cried as he walked slowly down the side of the road, feeling utterly exhausted and devastated.

> *"I will travel across the land,*
> *searching far and wiiiiiide.*
> *Teach Pokémon to understand*
> *the power that's insiiiiide. Pokémon!*
> *Gotta catch 'em all—it's you and meeee—"*

Suddenly, Pikachu started taking note of his surroundings. Something felt all too familiar. Pikachu's pace slowed even more. He realized he was at the bridge where he and Harry had suffered the fateful accident.

Pikachu trotted onto the bridge and found skid marks

that led to a large gap in the bridge's railing. Yellow caution tape hung across the opening with a temporary barrier set up behind it. Pikachu peered over the bridge onto the ground below, and saw the aftermath of an accident scene—a huge black spot surrounded by tire tracks left by emergency vehicles.

"I'm at the scene of the crash," Pikachu said.

Detective Pikachu flashed back to when he and Tim were in Howard's office and they watched the hologram of the crash. Now that he was at the site itself, his ace detective skills kicked in. Pikachu inspected the entire area, and spotted something sticking out of the cement. What was that? He reached down for one, pulling really hard, and managed to pluck it out with a sharp metallic *TINGG!* Pikachu immediately realized what it was: a Greninja star. That snapped Pikachu into hyper focus—his mind was swimming with details as he took inventory of everything.

"Roger must have sent the Greninja to cause a crash . . . which means . . . Mewtwo was trying to protect us? But why wouldn't Howard have shown us this in the hologram?" Pikachu's eyes widened with sudden panic as the puzzle pieces clicked togeter. Pikachu had to find Tim. Fast!

With renewed energy and purpose, Pikachu sprinted toward Ryme City.

CHAPTER
16

Back in Ryme City, Tim rushed into Howard's penthouse. "Howard! Mr. Clifford!" Tim yelled. "Your son . . . has Mewtwo."

But Tim stopped dead in his tracks when he realized what he was seeing. It was not what he was expecting. Howard was wearing the same complicated headgear that Tim had seen in the hologram at the PCL lab—the neural link. "Wait, what?" he cried, feeling totally confused.

"Tim. It's gonna be okay," Howard assured him.

Behind Howard was a new containment chamber— with Mewtwo trapped inside. As Tim watched, the chamber began to fill with purple "R" gas from tanks that were beneath the floor. As the gas hit Mewtwo, it convulsed wildly.

Tim noticed that a cable snaked along the floor from the containment chamber to the back of Howard's chair and then into the neural link itself. But before Tim could react, the entire setup glowed and pulsed with a rising burst of energy. Suddenly, Howard's body went limp and lifeless in his wheelchair. Then the containment chamber opened, and out floated Mewtwo—a powerful specter to behold.

"The transfer worked. My body is in the chair, but my mind is in Mewtwo," Mewtwo announced.

"Howard?" Tim asked, confused and horrified. Somehow, the "R" and the neural link had transferred Howard's mind into Mewtwo's body.

"I'm sorry I lied to you," admitted the altered Mewtwo. *"I needed you and Harry's Pikachu to lead me to Mewtwo."*

Suddenly, all the clues connected. Everything hit Tim all at once. "Mewtwo didn't cause the crash . . ." said Tim.

"All your father had to do was take the money and walk away. But he started snooping around. I had to stop him," explained Mewtwo.

Tim exploded. "You tried to kill him!"

Altered Mewtwo barked back at Tim with anger. *"I had no choice!"* Then it tried to implore Tim to see its side of things. *"He tracked the 'R' to the battles, found Dr. Laurent, and then he and his Pikachu helped Mewtwo escape."*

Tim made a mad dash for the elevator. But Mewtwo used its psychic powers to immobilize him and levitate him in the air.

CHAPTER 17

Outside the CNM building, throngs of people and Pokémon had amassed. Pokémon balloons were floating in line for the start of the parade, and a large stage sat in front of the CNM building. In front of the stage was a press pool that was cordoned off by police. The mayor of Ryme City was being interviewed.

"So, as you can see, we are more than happy with the turnout today. So many families—" the mayor's interview was cut short as he was summoned to the stage. "Thank you so much. Thank you. That's all for today. Thank you."

Lieutenant Yoshida sat on the stage with Snubbull on his lap. Next to him were the police chief, fire chief, city officials, business leaders, and their respective Pokémon. The mayor and his Doduo made their way onto the stage as Lucy pushed through the crowd wearing the red blazer she'd borrowed from Cynthia McMaster. "Excuse me, please. Hello!" she called out to the mayor.

Lucy proudly showed her CNM badge to the police officer at the barricade. "Hi. I have an interview with the mayor," she fibbed.

The police officer waved Lucy through. She entered the press pool and raced over to the mayor.

"Mr. Mayor! Mr. Mayor! I need to speak with you, please. It's urgent," Lucy called out frantically.

The mayor turned and Lucy immediately froze. Roger Clifford was standing right beside the mayor. "A little late for an interview, don't you think?" the mayor said.

"Please!" Lucy begged.

But the mayor just continued up the steps to the stage. Lucy was ready to pursue the mayor up the stairs, but then she realized that Roger had noticed her. She couldn't risk Roger finding out that she knew what he was up to. Lucy immediately backed away and disappeared into the crowd.

As the cameras went live, the mayor stepped up behind the podium. "Before we begin the parade, I'd like to thank our benefactor, Howard Clifford."

CHAPTER 18

Back at Clifford Tower, Tim was still suspended in midair, struggling in vain. He couldn't move from the neck down.

"Your father failed to understand my vision," the altered Mewtwo explained. *"Mewtwo has the power to transfer the soul of a human into the body of a Pokémon, as long as the Pokémon are in a crazed state. The 'R' gas takes care of that."*

As Tim hung in the air, the neural link on Howard's limp body caught his attention. His brain was working overtime trying to figure out what Mewtwo (or, really, Howard) was planning. He glanced out of the window onto the street and suddenly it all came together. "The balloons. The 'R' gas is in the balloons!"

Mewtwo was furious that Tim had put all the pieces

together. It hurled Tim across the room, where he slammed into the wall and fell to the floor, unconscious. With Tim out of the way, there was nothing else keeping altered Mewtwo from implementing its plan. Mewtwo shot a pulse of energy toward the window—shattering the glass. *Boom!*

The people and Pokémon on the streets below felt the impact of the mighty pulse of energy. Lucy was completely knocked back by its power. All eyes in the crowd turned skyward toward the noise and watched as the glass in the penthouse rained down onto the street. Gasps echoed through the crowd.

Lieutenant Yoshida immediately stood up, straining his eyes to see who was behind the scene that was unfolding. Lucy quickly tucked into the crowd as Mewtwo descended and hovered above the crowd.

It began to speak. *"People of Ryme City: I've finally discovered a cure. Not just for me, but for all of humanity. Pokémon can evolve into better versions of themselves, and now, so can you. Humans and Pokémon merged into one!"*

Mewtwo used its powers to open the valves on the balloons, releasing plumes of purple "R" gas over the crowd.

"Don't let your Pokémon breathe the purple gas!" Lucy

tried to warn everyone around her as she retreated down the street.

But no one listened. And as the gas hit the crowd, all the Pokémon started to go absolutely crazy!

"This is Yoshida requesting backup," called the lieutenant into his walkie-talkie. "All units should proceed to—"

Yoshida's call for help was cut off. As the gas hit Snubbull, it went from grumpy to grumpy on steroids! Yoshida struggled to hold Snubbull at arm's length as it snarled wildly at him.

Mewtwo fired a purple aura of energy from its outstretched arms. It washed over the crowd below. Suddenly, Yoshida and everyone else on the stage who was struggling with their Pokémon collapsed and disappeared. Their minds were entering their Pokémon! A moment later, an altered Snubbull stood up, looking totally confused.

Lucy raced down the street, warning anyone and everyone in her path. "Don't let your Pokémon breathe the gas! Don't let your Pokémon breathe the gas!"

Cynthia McMaster stood frozen in place in front of her cameraman and stared at the chaos unfolding a block away. *Wham!* Cynthia was suddenly bodychecked by Lucy and pushed out of the view of the camera. Lucy straightened up, grabbed the mic, looked right at the camera, and started broadcasting. "This is Lucy Stevens, reporting a citywide emergency! DO NOT let your Pokémon breathe the— Psyduck! No, Psyduck, don't—"

Lucy's attention was broken as Psyduck exited her car and waddled toward her. She dropped the mic and rushed over to it, but it was too late. A cloud of "R" hit Psyduck, and it went totally nuts. Then Mewtwo fired another purple aura of energy. Lucy collapsed and disappeared—and Psyduck found itself hosting Lucy's mind.

The altered Psyduck turned back to the camera and uttered all it could say: *"Psyduck?"*

CHAPTER 19

Detective Pikachu ran as fast as he possibly could. At long last, he finally arrived on the streets of Ryme City—and then stopped short. Ahead of him were hundreds of crazed Pokémon, deranged from the effects of "R" and the altered Mewtwo.

"Okay. Worst parade I've ever seen," Pikachu declared.

That was when Pikachu noticed that there were no people anywhere. There were only Pokémon—Pokémon and mayhem. Pikachu started to run again, passing dozens of Pokémon.

Then, a familiar sound caught Pikachu's attention and stopped him in his path. *"Psyduck!"*

Pikachu turned to see a Psyduck holding a CNM

microphone and shouting into a camera on a tripod. But at the sound of Psyduck's voice, Pikachu realized that this wasn't the Psyduck that he once knew.

"LUCY?!" cried Pikachu. "What happened to you? Where's Tim?"

The altered Psyduck gestured wildly as it told Pikachu all about what had happened since they went their separate ways. *"PSYDUCK! PSYDUCK! PSYDUCK!"*

"Howard *is* Mewtwo? The neural link . . . Yeah, this was his plan all along!" Pikachu realized.

Psyduck pointed to the top of Clifford Tower. Pikachu knew that trying to stop Howard was going to be a fight. But he also knew that he had to do it.

Detective Pikachu stealthily climbed up to the top of a Gengar balloon and gave himself a pep talk. *"I want to be the very best—in a world we must defend! Pokémon! Gotta catch 'em all!"* he sang. "My powers are somewhere in here . . . come on. I just need a little spark to get this party started. Let's do this, Pikachu!"

With the power of Thunderbolt, Pikachu blasted the Gengar balloon as he leaped onto another balloon floating nearby. The Gengar balloon exploded into a giant fireball!

That caught the altered Mewtwo's attention, and it

zeroed in on Pikachu. *"That's Harry's Pikachu!"*

As Pikachu got to his feet on the balloon, he looked up to see something coming in fast and hot—Mewtwo! Mewtwo flew like a speeding bullet toward Pikachu, keen to get rid of him once and for all. It growled, *"You think you can stand in the way of the future? I am the future!"*

Then it sent a blast of energy, which knocked Detective Pikachu off of the balloon . . . and onto a giant Pikachu balloon.

"Thanks, giant me!" Pikachu said as he zapped the Pikachu balloon and leaped off. As the balloon exploded, Pikachu landed on a rooftop.

But Mewtwo followed him relentlessly. It attacked Pikachu yet again—but Pikachu managed to dodge it as he jumped off the rooftop, landing on the back of a Pidgeot that was flying past.

Meanwhile, inside Howard's penthouse, Tim had regained consciousness. He got up from the floor slowly. Feeling disoriented and wondering what he missed, Tim surveyed the situation. When he looked out the window, Tim could hardly believe his eyes. He saw Pikachu riding on the back of a Pidgeot. "He's back!" Tim exclaimed.

But Mewtwo was still pursuing Pikachu. *"Humanity is doomed. I am its cure—do you understand?"*

Tim could see that his partner was in trouble and needed his help. He turned away from the window, and focused on Howard's human body—lying unconscious in his chair. "The neural link . . ." he murmured, trying to brainstorm what to do next.

Tim's concentration was broken by a noise in the penthouse. There was a banging sound coming from the closet just to his left. Tim went over and swung open the door. Much to his surprise, a bound and gagged Roger Clifford fell out onto the floor.

"Roger?" Tim asked as he quickly removed the gag.

"Behind you," Roger warned Tim.

Tim slowly turned around and came face-to-face with . . . another Roger. This Roger was wearing the big, ugly designer sunglasses Tim had seen before. But then this Roger shape-shifted into Ms. Norman, the woman in the dark suit who'd brought them to CNM.

"You're a Ditto," Tim realized, just as Ms. Norman shape-shifted again. This time the shift was into the Pokémon's true form: Ditto. But then the Ditto switched into a Loudred—and immediately used it powers to blow Tim backward.

While Tim was taking on the shape-shifted Ditto

inside the penthouse, outside, Pikachu was still trying to use Pidgeot to outfly the altered Mewtwo. "Bank left! Bank right! Where did you learn to fly, the ground?" he bellowed at the Pokémon. "Remember your training! And yes, I'm backseat driving—it's trying to kill us!"

As Tim recovered from one Ditto attack, it approached to attack again. Tim begged it to stop. "No, no, no. Stop, stop! Wait, wait, wait."

But then Ditto shape-shifted again—it decided to play some mind games on Tim, and transformed into Lucy. "Come on! No, that's not fair," pleaded Tim. He knew in the back of his mind that the Ditto wasn't Lucy, but it would still be really hard to fight something that looked just like her.

The Ditto didn't wait for Tim to make the first move. It came in and hit Tim hard.

"Okay, for the record, I have no guilt hitting a beady-eyed version of the woman I am very attracted to," Tim claimed, trying to believe it himself.

Smack! The shape-shifted Ditto hit Tim yet again, this time with a roundhouse kick that sent him flying back.

Outside, Detective Pikachu continued to fly on the back of Pidgeot as Mewtwo attacked from behind.

"Pull up! Pull up! And don't breathe the gas," Pikachu directed Pidgeot. But then he noticed that something was different about Pidgeot. He sighed. "You breathed the gas, didn't you?"

Pikachu had hit the nail on the head. Pidgeot started going wild, soon shaking Pikachu off its back. He fell and landed on a nearby rooftop.

Inside the penthouse, Tim picked up a floor lamp and wielded it like a sword. Ditto responded by shifting into a Machamp. Just then, Mewtwo appeared outside the broken penthouse window and ordered the still-shape-shifted Ditto to finish off Tim. It responded by punching Tim so hard that Tim went flying out the window.

He managed to grab ahold of the windowsill on his way down, and was hanging on for dear life. "Ahhh! Help!" Tim yelled.

Pikachu, on a rooftop below, was not in great shape. But he spotted Tim dangling from the window of the Clifford Tower penthouse and cried out to him. He had to help his partner!

As Tim dangled from the windowsill, the Ditto transformed again, this time into Cubone. It pounded Tim's hands on the windowsill with its bone until Tim's left hand let go. The only thing between Tim and a brutal fall to the ground was his right hand. Tim needed help, and fast.

He looked around and spotted Detective Pikachu in the distance. "Pikachu!" he cried, hoping against hope that his partner could hear him and come to his rescue.

Just as Pikachu was picking himself up, Mewtwo approached. *"Harry's son is finished."*

There was no way Pikachu was going to leave Tim hanging—he just had to get through Mewtwo first. He conjured a massive attack. "Volt Tackle!" Pikachu cried out as it charged at Mewtwo. The Volt Tackle threw Mewtwo into the side of Clifford Tower.

But that left Pikachu totally spent. "Tim . . ." he called out as he collapsed to the ground. Tim watched helplessly as he dangled one-handed from the windowsill.

The Ditto, still shifted into Cubone, was back for more. It once again used its bone, this time to pound Tim's right hand. "Ahhh!" Tim cried out in pain.

Just when it looked like Tim couldn't take it anymore and was going to drop, Roger suddenly appeared behind the shape-shifted Ditto, holding a lamp above his head. He crashed the lamp down as hard as he could, making a direct hit to the Pokémon and sending it flying.

Then Roger leaned down and pulled Tim safely back into the penthouse.

"What kind of Ditto was that!?" asked an exhausted Tim, grateful to be alive.

"That was one of my father's genetic experiments," admitted Roger sadly.

Suddenly, the Ditto—transformed into a Braviary—came through the open window. It shifted again into a Bouffalant as it landed, crashing into Roger and sending him across the room. Roger hit his head and was knocked unconscious.

The Ditto then changed appearance again, this time into a Charizard. Tim backed against the containment chamber as the shape-shifted Ditto attacked. Tim dodged just in time, took a canister of "R," and blasted it into the Pokémon's face.

The shape-shifted Ditto inhaled the "R" and started to go wild. It transformed at lightning speed into eight different Pokémon, one after another, faster and faster, until it deflated into a puddle. Tim sighed in relief.

Outside, altered Mewtwo picked up a totally vulnerable Pikachu from the rooftop and flew into the air. Then, it began to conjure a massive purple energy attack, to deliver a death blow.

"*A feeble effort*," proclaimed Mewtwo to Pikachu. "*A Pikachu cannot defeat Mewtwo in battle.*"

Pikachu looked over to the penthouse, where Tim was standing at Howard's chair grabbing hold of the cable connecting the neural link. "I didn't need to defeat you," Pikachu replied. "I just needed to distract you. And I did."

"No!" Mewtwo screamed as it spun around and saw Tim yank the neural link off Howard's head. Howard's eyes popped open. He was back in his human body, in his wheelchair. "What have you done!?" he demanded.

Meanwhile, Detective Pikachu had dropped down onto a giant Mr. Mime balloon. He was absolutely spent, without an ounce of energy left. He slid down the balloon and fell off—hurtling through the sky toward the ground. Knowing his time was up, Pikachu closed his eyes and prepared for impact.

Tim watched Pikachu fall in the distance. "Pikachu! No!" he cried.

But then, Pikachu halted midair. Mewtwo had stopped him. Now that the neural link was broken, Mewtwo had regained consciousness and was back in control of its own body. "*I am myself again. Thanks to you,*" Mewtwo said to Tim.

Mewtwo ripped the neural link off its head as it and Pikachu gently floated back down to the ground.

Tim made his way out of the building and ran across

the street. "Pikachu!" he cried, "Are you okay?" He was relieved to see his partner again.

"Tim!" Pikachu responded, just as relieved. "I pushed you away and left you when you needed me, and I'm so very sorry for that," he said.

"I'm just happy you're back, partner," said Tim. All was forgiven.

Pikachu smiled and looked out at the city. Then he turned back to Mewtwo. "Please tell me you can fix all this . . ."

"*I will undo what has been done*," said Mewtwo.

Mewtwo floated benevolently above the streets, which were still full of chaos. Then, Mewtwo emitted the biggest blast of purple energy yet. It washed over the entire crowd . . . bringing the humans back, and restoring their minds. Pokémon were Pokémon once again.

Yoshida awoke with a start and found himself staring face-to-face with his snorting Snubbull.

Lucy woke up and exchanged a knowing look with Psyduck. "Let's never do that again," she said. Psyduck agreed.

Several hours later, the police were up in the CNM penthouse, hard at work logging evidence at the crime scene. Two cops wheeled out Howard, under arrest. Tim, Pikachu, Lucy, Psyduck, and Roger Clifford watched as Howard was taken away.

Roger turned to Tim. "The strange thing is, no matter what his flaws, deep down I blame myself for not being there for him."

"I'm sorry," said Tim.

"You!" Roger said, suddenly turning toward Lucy. "You were working on this story. You had a lead on it before anyone else even knew, right?"

"That's correct," Lucy answered, proudly.

"Good. Right," said Roger. "You're going on camera. I want you giving an in-depth report for CNM tonight, prime time. And make sure you close with, 'Roger Clifford pledges to undo all the harm his father caused. Starting with the Pokémon he experimented on.'"

As Roger left them, Lucy was left glowing. "I can't believe it," she said. We did it!"

"Psyduck!" Psyduck said excitedly to Pikachu.

"Calm down," Pikachu said to Psyduck. "We don't need you blowing up the city right after we saved it."

"Meet me later tonight?" suggested Lucy.

"Cool, I mean—yeah." said Tim.

"Okay," said Lucy as she turned and ran down the street with Psyduck in tow.

Tim and Pikachu were left alone. Pikachu gave Tim a little punch to say *"Way to go!"*

A purple light hit them and they turned around to find Mewtwo descending in front of them. *"There is one last thing I must fix,"* Mewtwo admitted.

"My father," Tim answered hopefully.

"The father you have been looking for has been with you all along," Mewtwo explained.

"What's he talking about?" asked Detective Pikachu.

Then Tim and Pikachu turned to each other in disbelief. "I don't . . ." Tim started but was at a loss for words.

Whoosh! Mewtwo hit them with purple energy. They were warped back into a flashback—back to the car crash again.

Mewtwo floated down from the sky to the scene of the crash and the huddled figures of Harry and Pikachu. Harry was barely moving. *"Pika . . . Pikachu!"* said Pikachu.

"You've done well, Pikachu," responded Mewtwo. *"Humanity is evil. But you have shown me that not all humans are bad. Harry Goodman, your Pikachu offers its body to save your mind. There is a son. With the son's return, I can repair the father. Your memory will be gone, but your heart will know who you are. I*

take this body so that you might live. Return with the son."

With that, Mewtwo floated away from Pikachu with Harry's limp body. A purple glow surrounded both Harry and Pikachu.

The flashback ended, and Tim and Pikachu shared a shocked look. They couldn't believe it. All this time, Harry and Pikachu had been one.

CHAPTER
20

Tim stood alone outside the entrance to the Tahnti train station. He stared out at the glistening city. Pokémon were everywhere. Everything and everyone was back the way it was supposed to be. Tim took out his phone and checked the time.

"Hey, kid," called a familiar voice. But it wasn't Detective Pikachu—it was Harry Goodman, Tim's father. Tim turned to see his dad in his true form—a handsome gumshoe with some swagger—walking toward him. Pikachu was beside him on all fours, just as it was supposed to be.

"Grams will meet you when you arrive," said Harry. Then he handed a train ticket to Tim, who nodded and stared down at it. The two of them shared a look, but were at a loss for words.

"I'll see ya," said Harry, clearly sad to see his kid leave.

"See ya," said Tim back, flooded with emotion.

They hugged, and Tim turned and walked toward the station entrance. Harry watched him go, heartbroken.

Pikachu turned to Harry, feeling the same way. "*Pika.*"

Just before Tim entered the station door, he hesitated, and then turned back. He wasn't ready to go. He wasn't ready to say goodbye.

"Hey, Dad," said Tim.

"Yeah!" Harry replied.

"You think I can stay with you for a while?" Tim asked.

Harry couldn't believe it. He'd been waiting for Tim to want to spend time with him for as long as he could remember. He wanted that more than anything in the world. "I'd like that, kid. I'd like that very much," he said, happily.

"Me too," admitted Tim.

Tim threw the train ticket in the trash, and he and his father headed back into the streets of Ryme City. Pikachu bounced happily beside them.

"You want to get a coffee?" asked Tim.

"It's the weirdest thing. All I've been thinking about is having a coffee right now," said Harry, smiling.

"I think I'll have to find a new job," Tim realized.

"Oh, yeah?" asked Harry. "What are you thinking?"

"Maybe I could give detective work a try," Tim suggested.

"*Pika, pika!*" responded Pikachu.

"I think he likes that idea," said Harry. He put his arm around his son's shoulders, and they walked away together.